Easy Come, Easy Ghost

THE GHOST DETECTIVE MYSTERIES - BOOK 8

JANE HINCHEY

BAYWOLF PRESS

BP

BAYWOLF PRESS

Baywolf Press

PO Box 43

Ingle Farm, SA, 5098

Australia

CHAPTER ONE

"*N*ervous?" Galloway watched as I punched the call button to summon the flight attendant for the third time.

"Pft, as if." It was, of course, a lie. How could I not be nervous about meeting his parents? When I first met Kade Galloway, his folks were safely tucked away on the other side of the world, living their best lives in Australia. Only now, they were not. Now they had an apartment in the Torres Place Retirement Community, Chicago. But I wasn't really *nervous* about meeting them. I'd moved beyond nervous and into terrified. What if they hated me?

"Ma'am?" The attendant arrived, all white smiles and red lipstick, her hair pulled back in a perfect bun without a single strand escaping. I touched a hand to my hair. Had I even brushed it today?

"I'll have another, please." I smiled back, holding my empty cup toward her. She took it with a tight smile, pressed my call button, and promised to be back shortly.

"Another?" The man sitting to my left snorted. "That much caffeine can't be good for you."

"Here's hoping."

Galloway's hand landed on my thigh, making me jump. "Everything okay?"

"Fine. Everything's fine." Everything was not fine. For a start, we'd left home at the crack of dawn to drive to the airport to catch flight SA0321 to Chicago. I did not do crack of dawn well. Galloway had been a sweetheart, prepping me for the day with caffeine, carrying our bags, driving the hour-long journey to the airport, and paying for short-term parking.

"I hate to see the shape of your liver," the guy on my left continued with his uninvited criticism. "High levels of caffeine can hinder the liver's function."

"You didn't tell me you were afraid of flying," Galloway said from my right. My head was swiveling back and forth so fast I was getting dizzy. Or maybe it was the caffeine. Or that I was thirty-four thousand feet in the air with a dead guy running commentary on my lifestyle choices. It wasn't so much that my seat neighbor was deceased that had me rattled. But the dead guy sitting in seat 17F? He was missing half his head. *I know!* I was freaked out, too.

And if that weren't bad enough (believe me, it was!), but Dead Guy? He had friends. There had to be at least a dozen ghosts on the flight with us—all of them sporting gruesome injuries. Some were missing limbs. It was the worst in-flight entertainment ever.

"I'm not afraid of flying," I assured Galloway, placing my hand over his on my thigh. "I'm afraid of crashing."

"Babe, flying is perfectly safe."

I snorted. "Yeah? Tell him that." I jerked my head toward Dead Guy. Galloway peered around me, eyeballing the empty seat. "We have company?" He lowered his voice so we wouldn't be overheard.

"Do we ever," I confirmed. "And from the look of him, I'm going to hazard a guess that he went down in a plane crash."

"That bad, huh?"

"Worse."

The flight attendant returned with my drink.

After accepting the steaming cup, I turned to the dead guy and said, "This is my last one." It was really difficult not to stare at his disfigured face. Instead, I focused my attention on the window and the blue skies beyond.

"Hey." Dead Guy threw his hands in the air. "Don't let me stop you."

"I thought that was the whole point?" Despite telling myself not to engage, I engaged. "That, according to you, I drink too much coffee. Not that you know the first thing about me," I added under my breath.

"Uh, babe?" Galloway squeezed my knee hard, drawing my attention to the audience across the aisle, watching as I talked to an empty seat. Sighing, I took a hefty gulp of my beloved beverage of choice, not caring about the searing heat burning my esophagus.

Lifting the armrest between us, Galloway wrapped his arm around my shoulders and tugged me against his side in a comforting embrace. As much as my seatbelt would allow, anyway. "Sorry," I whispered. "Here. Want this?" I held my cup out to him, and he chuckled. "Nope. That's all yours. And I'm not annoyed at you drinking coffee. Have another if you want. You're obviously seeing something distressing... I'm assuming not your usual ghost?"

"Not at all." My usual ghost was *whole*, for want of a better word. I'd never had such a ghoulish ghost before. And I most certainly hadn't been prepared for his entourage, that's for sure.

"What happened to you, anyway?" I asked the dead guy, ignoring the folks across the aisle who were whispering to themselves, no doubt passing judgement on the crazy chick in seat 17E.

"What do you mean?" Dead Guy leaned forward to peer around me. "See? They don't approve of you drinking so much coffee, either."

I snorted, a loud, unladylike sound. "Dude, they're seeing me talking to thin air. They think I'm certifiable."

It was Dead Guy's turn to snort. "Lady, you're clearly off your meds. You're making no sense."

"Babe?" Galloway gave me another warning squeeze, reminding me—again—that I had an audience to my one-sided conversation.

"Sorry," I muttered, finishing my coffee and placing the cup on my fold down tray. "Maybe I'll try to nap."

"Brilliant idea." Dead Guy nodded. "I'll do the same."

Leaning my head against Galloway's shoulder, I shut my eyes, but as much as I yearned for sleep, it was not to be, for now my bladder was telling me those three coffees I'd had in quick succession were searching for an exit. Sitting upright, I unsnapped my seatbelt. "I need to pee."

Galloway released his seatbelt and stood, a steadying hand on my arm that didn't prevent me from smacking my head straight into the overhead locker. "Ouch. You okay?"

"Fine," I said through gritted teeth, feeling my cheeks heat as everyone turned to look. "I'm fine." Smoothing my T-shirt into place, I noticed a small wet spot where I'd dripped some coffee. I rubbed at it, as if it would magically dry and disappear. Stepping into the aisle, I made my way toward the bathrooms at the back of the plane, figuring the shirt would dry by the time we landed and Galloway's family wouldn't notice one small stain. I could hear the deep timbre of Galloway's voice behind me, no doubt assuring everyone I was not some deranged psychopath.

I hustled into the cupboard they called a bathroom and locked the door, thankful to have a moment to myself.

"Get yourself together, Audrey," I whispered,

running my hands over my face. The coffee had seemed like a good idea at the time, but now I was second-guessing my life choices because my hands were trembling and I felt... twitchy. Caffeine overload, for sure. I was meeting Galloway's family in—I glanced at my watch—one hour. Hopefully, the effects of the caffeine rush would fade by then.

I'd finished peeing but remained seated, pondering my options, when something happened that had never, ever happened before.

A ghost appeared. Not so unusual, right? But this woman? She appeared in me! Or I was in her. Either way, she was heart freezingly cold! Shards of ice shot through my body, generally shocking as a whole because I was sitting on the toilet, and so was she. I couldn't help it. I screamed. She screamed. And then there was banging on the bathroom door and someone asking, "Is everything all right in there?"

Slapping my hand over my mouth, I jumped to my feet, trying to get away from the ghost, which was tough in such tight quarters, especially with my jeans and underwear around my knees. "What the hell?" I hissed at the woman, who, for all intents and purposes, appeared to be peeing. I turned my back, tugging my clothing back into position to cover my bare butt.

"Do you *mind?*" Her voice dripped with disdain. "This bathroom is occupied."

"Yes," I hissed back. "By me! I was here first, lady!"

Someone banged on the door again. "Miss? Are you okay?"

"Yes, I'm fine." I called out, then glared at the ghost, who merely smirked and shrugged her shoulders. Holding her gaze, I defiantly slapped my hand on the flush button, hoping—rather maliciously—that she'd get sucked to wherever toilet waste gets sucked to on a plane. Alas, she remained in situ, returning my glare. I washed and dried my hands, unlocked the door, and stepped outside, forcing the flight attendant to back up a step. "Oh, sorry," I automatically apologized, even though she'd been the one standing right outside the door, blocking my exit.

"Are you okay, miss?" she asked, eyeing me up and down. "Can I get you anything?"

Xanax? Valium, perhaps? "I'm fine."

"Do you need a hand getting back to your seat?" she offered, and my face burned with embarrassment. I wasn't sure if she thought I was drunk, drug addled, or just unsteady on my feet, and to be fair, who could blame her? I was the clumsiest person I knew. But one little scream in the bathroom hardly warranted an escort back to my seat.

"I'm fine," I repeated, and to prove it, I made it all the way back to my seat without stumbling once, despite having to walk directly through a ghost blocking the aisle.

CHAPTER TWO

I was sweating. I could feel it pooling beneath my boobs. I tugged at my bra, then fanned my face. We were standing at the carousel waiting for our luggage. Galloway had smoothed things over with the folks seated around us, and I'd promptly fallen asleep despite the caffeine surging through my body, therefore blocking out the ghosts haunting flight SA0321.

Galloway glanced at me, then did a double take. "Okay?" he asked, brushing my hair back from my face. I figured I looked as bad as I felt.

I gritted my teeth and smiled. "I'm fine."

"They're going to love you," he reassured me, his touch comforting. I automatically leaned my cheek into his palm, like a kitten seeking affection. He chuckled and dropped a kiss on my nose before turning his attention back to the carousel.

"I am a little concerned," I admitted. "Not so much about meeting your family. But it's where they live." It had occurred to me on the plane, surrounded by the ghosts who were stuck in some ghastly time loop, reliving their last moments before they'd perished in what I assumed to be an airplane crash, that I may just be walking into a similar situation with his folks.

"Oh?" He didn't turn around, his eyes scanning over the luggage that had appeared, searching for our bags.

"The Torres Place Retirement Community?" I prompted, hoping he'd get the hint, for I couldn't very well say I was worried that his parents' apartment was haunted by the ghosts of previous residents given we were shoulder to shoulder with fellow passengers all jostling to get their bags.

He shot a look over his shoulder. "Oh!" He got it. The Torres Place Retirement Community on the banks of Lake Michigan was huge, sporting an apartment complex for independent living, plus a nursing home for those needing extra care. There was a gym, a pool, a nine-hole golf course, walking paths, a dining room that rivaled a five-star restaurant, and a salon. I'd googled it and pored over the pictures, and the place was a dream. But now I couldn't help but worry about how many of the un-living were residing there.

"Mom and Dad's place should be fine." He grunted, heaving a bag off the carousel and turning to place it at my feet. "The realtor has to disclose if anyone..." He paused and met my eyes. "You know. We're in the clear."

I sagged in relief. If no one had died in their apartment, it should, theoretically, be ghost free. Retrieving our other bag, he picked up both, and I trotted alongside as we left the airport.

"Was it bad then? On the plane?" he asked, heading toward the cab rank.

I nodded. "There was a lot. One even used the bathroom."

He stopped, and I walked straight past, taking a second or two to realize he was no longer by my side. "Is that what that commotion was about?" He caught up with me.

"Uh-huh." I sucked in a deep breath and released it in a whoosh. "I really want this to go smoothly, and I admit, I'm nervous about meeting your parents, so the last thing I need is ghostly interference."

"It'll be fine," he said, for the millionth time.

───────────

"Oh my God, Kade, she's gorgeous!" Sylvia Galloway clamped her hands on my shoulders and looked me up and down, her gray eyes identical to her son's. "Welcome, Audrey. We are so thrilled to finally meet you."

I cleared my throat. "Er, you too." Sylvia was a retired schoolteacher, with a colorful beaded chain dangling from the glasses perched on her nose. She wore a soft peach sweater with blue jeans and bare feet. She ushered us into the apartment.

"You sure it's okay for us to stay here, Mom?" Galloway kissed her cheek in greeting, carrying a bag in each hand.

"Of course, darling. We bought a three bedroom for this purpose. One for us, one as a den for your father, and a guest room. Or, you know, for future grandbabies."

"Mom." Galloway's voice held a warning growl.

I chewed my lip, wondering if he'd told them I wasn't even sure I wanted children. And even if I did, any mini Galloways were a looooooong way in the future.

"Relax, darling, stop your fussing." She shooed off his warning with a wink to me. "Audrey, come and meet Dennis. He's in the living room. You'll have to forgive him for not getting up to greet you, but as you can see, the entryway isn't very big and us Galloways aren't exactly small." She turned her attention to Kade and pointed. "Guest room is through there. Drop your bags and come and say hello to your father."

I allowed myself to be ushered into the open plan living, dining, and kitchen area. The kitchen itself was tiny, as was the dining area, but massive floor to ceiling windows in the living room with a spectacular view of Lake Michigan more than made up for it. "Wow!" I breathed. "That view is amazing."

Sylvia stood next to me, smiling. "Isn't it just? We love it here."

"And you must be Audrey."

I'd been so enamored by the view that I'd missed Kade's father, seated in a recliner by the window. He stood, weight balanced on a walking cane as he smiled at me, a dimple flashing in his cleanly shaven cheek. Kade Galloway was the spitting image of his father, with his mother's eyes.

I stepped forward and shook his hand,

unprepared when he pulled me in for a bear hug. "Pleased to meet you, Audrey."

"You too," I wheezed.

"Place looks great, Mom." Kade joined us, slapping his father on the back with a "Hi, Dad!"

"I was just telling Audrey how much we like it here." Sylvia beamed with pride. Turning to me, she explained, "We loved Australia, but it was time we came home. Dennis's war wound was making its presence felt now that he's a bit older, so we figured a place like this would be perfect. We still have our independence, but help is on hand should we need it."

"War wound? I didn't know you were in the army."

Dennis snorted. "Kade didn't tell you my heroic tale?"

I shook my head. "He told me you're a retired police officer."

"One of Chicago's finest," Kade added.

"Yeah, until I took a bullet to the leg. Shattered the bone. Retired on disability." He slapped his thigh. "That'll teach me to chase a perp down a blind alley. Son-of-a—"

"Dennis!" Sylvia warned with a waggle of her finger, sounding very much like a schoolteacher.

"Son-of-a-*gun*," Dennis corrected, winking at me. "Had a concealed weapon."

"I'm so sorry."

"Don't be. It's not your fault." Dennis's smile was warm and oh so comforting, just like his son's. Kade slid his arm around my waist, and I relaxed into him. Maybe this wasn't going to be so bad after all.

"Oh, hello. I didn't realize we had company!"

I turned to see an elderly woman dressed in white pants that ended just below the knee, matching cap, and navy and white argyle sweater and socks.

"Hi." I smiled, looking her up and down. "Off to play golf?"

"Sure am! It's a beautiful day for it. And who are you, dear? Do I know you?"

I figured she was maybe Kade's aunt, although he hadn't mentioned any other family would be in attendance today. She looked a few years older than Sylvia, but there wasn't any family resemblance that I could see. Maybe she was from Dennis's side of the family?

"I'm Audrey." I held out my hand.

"Are you golfing with us today, Audrey?" The woman moved closer to shake my hand. "Oh, where are my manners? I'm Joyce."

"Uh... Audrey?" Galloway's fingers gripped my shoulder at the same time Joyce's hand met mine, and a familiar shot of ice shot through my palm.

"Darn," I whispered, my chin sinking to my chest. This was not good. I'd blatantly engaged in conversation with a ghost right in front of Kade's parents. There was no way they could miss it. I shot Kade a panicked look, and the worry on his face confirmed my suspicions. I was screwed.

Sucking in a deep breath, I squared my shoulders and faced Sylvia and Dennis. "Sorry about that." I shrugged, not knowing how to explain what they'd just witnessed.

Sylvia clasped her hands together beneath her chin, her eyes sparkling. "You said she was special, sweetheart, but you never said she was clairvoyant!"

"Um, it's not something many people know," he replied sheepishly.

Sylvia ignored him, her attention on me. "Is someone here?"

I chewed my lip. I could either go all in or try to bluff my way out. If Ben were here, he'd tell me to take the path of least resistance—but he wasn't here. I'd forbidden him from coming in case I got caught talking with him by Kade's parents. *Oh, the irony!*

"Is that the time?" Joyce drew my attention back

to her. She was tapping the watch on her wrist. "It was lovely to meet you Audrey, but I've gotta run. We're about to tee off, and I don't want to be late." She hurried away, walking straight through the apartment door. I raised my hand in an automatic salute and then let it slowly drop to my side.

"Not anymore," I said to Sylvia. "She just left."

"She? Who was it, dear?"

Hitching a breath, I went all in. "Her name is Joyce. She plays golf."

"Are you saying our apartment is haunted?" Dennis asked, eyebrows battling to reach his receding hairline.

I shook my head. "No, not necessarily. I'm what you'd call a ghost magnet. They seem to find me wherever I am."

Galloway slid his arm around my shoulders and addressed his parents using his cop voice. "Mom. Dad. This has to stay between us, understand? This gift Audrey has? It can be a curse, and the last thing she needs is word getting out. Only a select few people know."

"How select?" Sylvia asked, one delicate brow arching.

"You're the third and fourth living people who know. The other person is my neighbor."

"You mean your own family doesn't know?" Sylvia clapped a hand over her mouth.

I shook my head. "No. And I want to keep it that way. They'd only worry."

She mimed locking her lips. "Your secret is safe with us. Isn't it, Dennis?"

Dennis shrugged. "Sure." He eased back into his recliner. "But the question is, who is Joyce? And how did she die?"

Sylvia turned to me, face alight. "You said she was playing golf? We need to go see who she was meeting!"

"Hold on a second." Kade held up a hand. "There is nothing to suggest foul play. No need to go storming in, guns blazing, investigating what y'all seem to think is a potential homicide."

I one hundred percent agreed with him. Only I had a sneaky suspicion the senior Galloways were correct—why else would Joyce's ghost have found me?

"No reason to suspect it isn't either, son," Dennis said. "Your pretty fiancée said it herself. She's a ghost magnet. And we all know ghosts hang around because they have unfinished business. And what's more unfinished than finding yourself suddenly murdered?"

CHAPTER THREE

"*H*ow is this even happening?" I hissed out the corner of my mouth as all four of us piled into the elevator.

Kade rested his hand on the nape of my neck and shrugged. "Beats me. I mean, Mom has always had an interest in psychics and clairvoyants and watches TV shows like *Murder, She Wrote* and *CSI*, plus she's an intelligent woman. It took her all of two seconds to put it together."

"Audrey?" Sylvia Galloway glanced at me over her shoulder. "Is there a problem?"

"None, other than me being here was meant for us getting to know each other, not investigating murders. If there even has been a murder," I hastened to add.

Dennis blurted out, "What better way to bond than to solve a mystery together?"

My eyes rolled to the back of my head as I groaned inwardly. Kade must have sensed my apprehension, because he gave my neck a sympathetic squeeze. I mean, I knew meeting his parents was going to be a challenge, but solving a mystery with them? What was next, an escape room? I had to admit, this was not what I expected, but who knew—maybe we'd all form a club and start solving crimes in our free time. It was all I could do not to burst into hysterical laughter.

While I pondered how things had gone spectacularly wrong, the elevator deposited us on the ground floor, and I followed the senior Galloways out.

"Golf course is this way." Dennis pointed his walking stick. "We can grab a cart."

Path of least resistance, Fitz. Ben's voice echoed in my head. "Okay."

Kade entwined his fingers with mine as we ambled our way through the apartment complex, listening as Sylvia pointed out things of interest. "I've made a booking for dinner here tonight," she said, pointing to the five-star restaurant I'd read about. "And of course, if you ever want a snack or a coffee or whatever, the Sunset Café is fabulous."

As I stepped into the Sunset Café, the stunning view of the golf course took my breath away. The warm hues of the sun streaming through the windows illuminated the space, casting a soft, golden glow across the cafe. The open doors allowed the scenic view to serve as the perfect backdrop for a relaxing meal with friends before enjoying a round of golf. The word idyllic sprang to mind, and if we weren't searching for a ghost, I'd be tempted to sit and order up something scrumptious while enjoying the ambience.

Half a dozen round tables, each adorned with vibrant red and white checkered tablecloths, signaled that the café was already bustling with patrons. With my eyes darting around the room, I scanned the sea of diners' faces, eagerly searching for Joyce amidst them. "She's not here," I whispered to Kade.

"Maybe she's on the course?" he suggested. "But we can check with the staff, see if she was here this morning. I'm betting they're pretty familiar with the regulars."

"Excellent suggestion, son." Dennis made a beeline for the counter, Sylvia hot on his heels. I tugged Kade to a halt.

"What's up?" he asked.

"Could it be that your folks are... bored? That maybe this *investigation*"—I air quoted—"is giving them a little excitement that was previously lacking?"

"They do seem overly enthusiastic," he agreed. "Settling back into a more sedate lifestyle after traveling around Australia is bound to take some getting used to. I'm sorry if they're coming across as over the top—they're not really like this."

"No, no, no, it's fine," I assured him. "This"—I waved a hand around—"isn't what I expected to happen. I was thinking afternoon tea, easy getting-to-know you conversation, maybe talk about the wedding. Not blow my cover immediately and then be searching for a woman's body."

Sylvia and Dennis were fully engrossed in their conversation with the server behind the counter, gesticulating wildly as they listened to his every word. He was pointing toward a table on the terrace outside.

"What's up, kids?" Sylvia returned while Dennis kept talking with the server and appeared to be taking notes. "Never mind. We have a lead!" She was positively glowing, her words running together she was talking so fast. "A resident named Joyce golfs here three times a week. She was here this morning with her two friends, Sally and Hazel. They ate on the terrace, then took a golf cart and headed onto the course."

I glanced at Kade, who grinned at his mom's enthusiasm. "Good work," he said.

Ignoring his compliment, she grabbed his hand, dragging him across the café, while I dutifully followed behind. "Come on, Dennis is organizing a buggy for us."

It was a beautiful day in Chicago; the sun was out, birds chirping in the trees and a barely there breeze bringing with it the scent of summer, and yet I felt cold inside. A sense of dread weighed heavily on me as we piled into the golf buggy, Kade and I in the back, Dennis behind the wheel, and Sylvia riding shotgun.

Kade squeezed my knee. "Okay?"

"I have a terrible feeling about this," I grumbled, shivers running down my spine.

"Hey now," Kade soothed, placing a comforting hand beneath my chin and gently lifting my face to meet his gaze. His expression was full of concern.

"We'll find Joyce and let the authorities handle it. You don't have to be a hero."

"Easy for you to say," I retorted with a sigh. "Normally, when a ghost appears to me, it becomes my problem whether I like it or not."

Kade leaned in to kiss me, and for a moment, I forgot about everything else. It was the perfect distraction, and I melted into him, wrapping my arms around his waist and losing myself in the warmth of his embrace. Just when I thought things couldn't get any better, the buggy suddenly lurched to a stop, and I almost tumbled off the bench seat.

"Well, that's one way to kill the mood," I joked, steadying myself against the sudden halt.

"Tee one!" Dennis declared.

Untangling myself from Kade, I turned my attention to the vista before us. Acres of green, dotted with buggies and golfers in various stages of play.

"I don't see her," I said, searching for any sign of Joyce.

"Let's move on," Sylvia told her husband. "Realistically, she could be anywhere on the course, but you'd think we'd have heard a commotion by now. Unless..." Sylvia swiveled to look at me. "Is Joyce fresh?"

"Fresh?"

"As in, newly dead. Or is she an old ghost? Maybe she didn't die today like we're assuming—in which case we're on a wild ghost chase."

"It's a nice day for a wild ghost chase." Dennis winked at her and planted his foot, jerking us into motion once more. I fumbled for my seat belt, securing it across my hips.

"Didn't the guy back there say he saw Joyce at breakfast this morning? With her friends?" Galloway said.

Sylvia swiveled to smile at her son. "Why yes, he did! Of course, silly me. She has to be fresh."

"I'm off my game," I said under my breath, but Kade heard me.

"You don't have a home court advantage, that's all," he whispered into my ear. "You've got this, babe. Just relax. Stop stressing."

Turning my head, I looked to check he didn't have two heads. *Stop stressing? Is he serious?*

I guess my face gave me away, for he snorted out a laugh and held up his hands in surrender. "Okay, okay, poor choice of words."

"Look!" Sylvia interrupted, pointing. "It looks like something is on the ground over there."

On the horizon was what appeared to be a set of

golf clubs lying on the ground. From this distance, I couldn't make out if Joyce's body was with them, but I'd be willing to bet money it was.

Leaning forward, I rested my hand on Dennis's shoulder. "Head that way."

He obliged, and the closer we got, the more I realized I was right. What I'd thought were golf clubs was actually Joyce herself. Well, the physical body of Joyce, for Joyce the ghost was standing next to her corpse and waving madly at me.

"Yoo-hoo! Good morning!" she called. "Decided to join us after all? It's a beautiful day for a round."

I groaned, and Kade shot me a look. "I don't think she realizes she's dead," I whispered in explanation.

"How could she not? Her body is right there!"

"What's that?" Sylvia half turned to ask.

"Joyce's ghost is here." Kade leaned forward, his hand resting on his mom's shoulder. "Remember, let Audrey do her thing, okay?"

Sylvia waved her son away as if he were a bothersome fly. "Of course. You don't have to keep telling me. I don't have dementia."

Dennis pulled the golf cart to a halt, grabbed his walking stick, and stiffly climbed out. Sylvia and Kade followed suit, and I went to join them, only to be jerked unceremoniously backward by the seat belt. Feeling my cheeks heat with embarrassment, I quickly unsnapped the buckle and practically fell out.

While everyone gathered around Joyce's body and Kade kneeled to check her pulse, I moved away, jerking my head for Joyce to follow me. Thankfully, she did.

"You know you're dead, right?" I asked bluntly. Usually, I approached the subject with more tact and diplomacy, but today was not usual, and time was not on my side.

Joyce sighed, her shoulders slumping. "I know. I mean, the sudden ability to walk through solid objects gave it away."

"Not to mention your body on the ground."

"That too," she agreed.

"So, what happened? Heart attack playing golf?" It was wishful thinking. If that had been the case, Joyce would most likely have moved on already, not been stuck earthbound in spirit form.

Joyce chewed a nail. "You know, it's the darndest thing..."

"Don't tell me. You don't remember?" Another common theme amongst the undead. Most of them didn't remember dying. Which made solving their murders challenging, but not impossible. In fact, I had quite the list of solved cases ever since I'd cracked the mystery of my best friend Ben's murder.

Joyce dropped her arm and looked at me. "The last thing I remember is having breakfast with Sally and Hazel."

"You don't remember getting in the buggy? Coming out onto the golf course?"

She shook her head.

"Any idea who would want you dead?"

Her hand fluttered to her throat, and a look of horror swept across her face. "Not at all! I'm a perfectly lovely person. Who would want to kill *me*?"

"That's what I intend to find out," I said, crossing my arms over my chest.

"You think I was *murdered*?" It was clear Joyce hadn't considered the prospect, yet why else was her ghost here, talking with me?

"Again, that's what I intend to find out."

"Who are you, anyway?"

"Audrey Fitzgerald, private investigator."

Joyce gave me a look that said she was clearly impressed. "I see you're with Dennis and Sylvia. And the man who's with you bears a striking family resemblance, so I'm guessing he's their son? Is he a private investigator too?"

"He's a detective," I replied. "I didn't realize you knew the Galloways. They only moved in recently."

"Oh, I don't *know* know them. I know *of* them. You know what the gossip mill is like. Someone new moves into the building, and everyone is all up in their business, finding out what's what."

I nodded. "Right."

Kade caught my eye and jerked his head toward Joyce's body.

"So, here's the thing, Joyce," I said in a rush. "I'm the only one who can see and hear you, so when there are other people around, I won't be able to respond, okay? This has to remain our little secret."

"Gotcha!"

I joined Kade, Joyce's body at our feet. Dennis moved away to put in a call to the authorities, Sylvia by his side.

"Take a closer look," Kade invited, crouching by Joyce's side. I mimicked his movements, wondering what, exactly, I was looking for, when, between one blink and the next, I saw it. Tire tracks.

I looked at Kade, aghast. "She was run over?" My eyes darted over his shoulder to the rolling green, straining to catch a glimpse of the buggy with her friends in it. Had Sally and Hazel run her over and then left, done a runner?

"These are definitely tread marks," Kade agreed. The marks themselves were not clearly visible, not dirty black marks like you see in the movies, more like a green scuff mark across Joyce's white Capri pants.

I looked at our golf buggy, to Joyce, and back again. "Okay, let's say she was run over... is a buggy heavy enough to actually kill her?" I slapped my hand against the buggy for emphasis, the action stinging my palm and making my eyes water.

Kade cocked his head and thought on it a minute before shrugging. "Ordinarily, I'd say no, but she's an old woman. More fragile. If the buggy ran over her chest, it could have exerted enough pressure to damage her heart."

I pointed to Joyce's legs. "But it ran over her legs. Not her torso. Look, no signs of tire tracks, only a—" I took a closer look at the argyle vest Joyce wore. "Is that... orange juice?" There was a small stain, barely noticeable.

"I'm a messy eater," Joyce confessed.

"Me too, Joyce, me too." I sighed.

Dennis finished up the call and returned to us. "Authorities are on the way. What do we have?"

"Deceased," Kade confirmed, straightening to a

standing position and taking my hand, his fingers curling around mine.

Dennis pointed his walking stick at Joyce's legs. "Hit and run?"

Kade shrugged, looking baffled. "She's definitely been run over, but whether that killed her? Hard to say."

"It would explain her ghost being here, though, right?" Sylvia said, looking from me to Kade and back again. "You said a sudden death made them hang around?"

"Possibly," I hedged, not wanting to definitively say one way or another that Joyce had been killed by a golf buggy.

CHAPTER FOUR

Kade kept a comforting hand on my shoulder while we watched the paramedics strap Joyce's body to a gurney. A man and woman in matching navy suits had followed the ambulance in a golf cart and were now speaking with Dennis and Sylvia. Joyce told me they were management, and she was pretty sure they were sleeping together.

"Second call out to Torres Place today," I overheard one paramedic say as they wheeled Joyce to the waiting ambulance.

"Hope it's not the start of a trend," the other replied before they'd moved past.

"Oh, that's right!" Joyce declared loudly into my ear, making me jump.

"You remember something?" I mumbled out of the corner of my mouth.

"Yes, yes. When the paramedics get called out multiple times in one day, it's considered a trend. Of deaths. I must be the second person who's died today. If there's a third, then..."

I gave her a slight nod to let her know I'd heard her but couldn't reply verbally because the two managers in their crisp suits were headed our way.

"Thank you for assisting in this unfortunate situation this morning," the woman said, smoothing her hands over her hips. "I'm Hayden Lee, head of HR, and this is Paul Wilson, chief operations manager."

"Chief schlepping manager, more like it," Joyce said sarcastically. I bit my tongue and did my best to ignore her.

Kade took over. "Detective Kade Galloway, Firefly Bay PD, and this is my fiancée Audrey and my parents, Sylvia and Dennis Galloway."

Hayden smiled a plastic smile. "Yes, we just met. How are you settling in?"

"I hardly think this is the best time to be asking, Hayden." Paul looked down his nose at the woman by his side. If they were sleeping together, I'd be a monkey's uncle. It wasn't a look of love, lust, or even a remote speck of attraction that crossed Paul's face as he glared at the pretty redhead by his side. If anything, it was disdain and dislike.

Hayden blushed. "Of course. My apologies."

"Not at all," Dennis said. "A perfectly reasonable question under the circumstances, I would think. We're new here. Hayden was asking how we were settling in. Hardly a crime. What is a crime is what happened on the golf course today."

"You think this woman's death is a crime?" Paul's eyebrows shot up, and he glanced toward the ambulance that was preparing to depart.

"Any unexplained death should be treated as suspect, don't you agree?" Dennis said.

Paul smoothed down the lapels of his suit and looked down his nose. "You have to understand that in a facility such as Torres Place, deaths are not only inevitable, they are frequent. Dare I say, expected."

"Are you telling *me*," Dennis shot back, his face flushing and his hands clenching into fists, "that you don't review any of your deaths? That you assume they are simply age or illness related?"

Kade apparently noticed his father growing increasingly upset, and he gently rested a hand on his dad's shoulder. "It's okay, Dad. We'll get to the bottom of this. We'll find out what happened."

I met Kade's worried gaze, suggesting, "Perhaps we should head back? I wouldn't mind taking a break and having a cup of coffee." It wasn't entirely untrue, but I also sensed Dennis was flagging, possibly in pain but too stubborn to admit it.

"Great idea," Dennis boomed, rallying. "I could use a brew, and we can regroup."

"That's settled then." Sylvia began ushering us toward the golf buggy we'd hired. "Let's stop at the Sunset Café for refreshments."

As we piled into the buggy, my mind couldn't help but conjure up images of frothy cappuccinos and fluffy cupcakes, tantalizing my taste buds. However, my appetite was quickly dampened when I cast a last glance over my shoulder and noticed Paul and Hayden standing there, watching us intently. Paul Wilson's stony gaze could have seared through steel, and it was unmistakably directed at us.

As I locked eyes with him, I felt a shiver run down my spine. Then his expression softened as he muttered something to Hayden, gesturing toward their own buggy. It was clear they were heading in the same direction as us, but the thought of being in such close proximity to Paul made me uneasy.

"Everything okay?" Kade murmured in my ear, and I leaned against him, taking comfort from his presence.

"I'm really worried something is off here," I whispered, keeping my voice low so his parents wouldn't overhear. "I'm getting a really bad vibe from Paul."

Kade's brows shot up. "You think he's involved in Joyce's death?"

"I mean... what are the chances? I've already dealt with one angel of death..." I trailed off, remembering a previous case, one where one of the nurses at a retirement home much smaller than Torres Place was killing the residents. But in that case, it wasn't one ghost dogging my heels. There had been dozens.

"That's a pretty serious accusation."

I jerked myself back to the present. "No, I know." I sighed. "He's probably not involved at all. I just got a nasty vibe from him. And that's not a crime."

"Are there more ghosts?" Kade pressed, glancing across the green as if he could see them for himself. Which he couldn't because A) he couldn't see ghosts and B) there were no ghosts to see.

"Nope. Just Joyce, and she's disappeared. For now."

Outside of the Sunset Café stood a row of golf buggies, and Dennis zipped into a parking spot at the end, jerking to a stop with a little squeal of the tires.

Sylvia turned to face us, leaning over the back of the seat. "Sorry for his driving. He's not allowed to drive anymore, you see, so when he does get behind the wheel, he's a tad enthusiastic."

"It's not that I'm not allowed to drive," Dennis grumbled, swinging his legs out of the buggy before retrieving his walking stick. "More that I can't. Physically. I haven't lost my license like she makes it sound."

"Fine." Sylvia rolled her eyes, then shot me a wink and mouthed "men!"

Following Kade's parents into the café, I said to Kade, "Should he have been driving the golf buggy even? His pain seems to be worse."

It was Kade's turn to heave a sigh. Worry for his father flashed in his eyes, and I squeezed his hand in support. "A buggy is much lighter than a car, easier to control. I'm not going to argue with him over it. If he wants to drive it, he can drive it."

I was shocked by his tone. Kade wasn't one to get snippy. In fact, he was the most laid back person I knew. Not much fazed him. "Babe." I didn't know what to say, but I guess my tone belayed my sentiments, for he drew to a stop and tugged me into his arms, engulfing me in an embrace.

"Sorry," he grumbled in my ear. "I'm not used to seeing him like this."

"It sucks." I had no personal experience to draw on. Both my parents were in good health, but then there was Ben's dad, whom I was now responsible for since Ben died. Poor Bill Delaney suffered terribly with Alzheimer's and spent his days living in the past. It was kinda the same, but different.

Stepping over the threshold, I stumbled while my eyes struggled to adjust from the bright day outside to the relative dimness of the café. When I could finally focus again, I saw the same man behind the counter who Dennis and Sylvia had talked to earlier waving us over.

"Mom, Dad, grab us a table. I'll see what he wants," Kade said.

I figured Kade didn't need me trotting along behind like an abandoned puppy, so I took a seat with the senior Galloways, not missing Dennis popping a pill as soon as he was seated.

"Are you okay?"

He shot me a rueful grin. "Sorry if I'm being a grump."

"It's his leg," Sylvia added.

"The more it aches, the grumpier I get."

"He hates the way it slows him down. That makes him grumpy too," Sylvia chimed in, but the loving look she shared with her husband took any sting out of her words.

"It sure does," he agreed, then leaned toward his wife. She met him halfway, the quick kiss they shared showing how much they loved each other, grumpy or not.

Kade returned, pulling out the chair next to mine. "I ordered for us. Hope you don't mind?"

"As long as there's a coffee in my immediate future, I don't mind at all," I said.

"What did he want?" Dennis asked, jerking his head toward the server.

"He wanted to let you know that the ladies you were asking about this morning, the ones out golfing with Joyce? The other two returned without her a few minutes ago. They're sitting over there." Keeping his hand low, he pointed to a table across the room where two seniors sat. Of course, we all swiveled in our seats and gawked at them. The women didn't notice us, too busy having an animated conversation, arms waving around but keeping their voices low enough that their fellow diners couldn't overhear.

Both women were decked out for golfing. One wore a teal polo shirt, straw sun visor, and large sunglasses, while the other wore a navy sleeveless button-down and reading glasses.

"Why is she wearing her hat and sunglasses indoors?" Sylvia asked what I was thinking.

"They look shifty." Dennis squinted at the women, cop brain working overtime. He made a move as if to stand, but Sylvia slapped her fingers around his wrist, keeping him in his seat.

"No," she scolded. "You need to rest. And don't you go arguing with me, Dennis Galloway. We both know that little jaunt around the golf course took it out of you, and if you don't want to be sent upstairs for a nap, you'll keep your tush in that chair and let your son do the investigating just this once. Kade, tell your father you'll report back every single word they say."

"Dad, I've got this covered. Mom's right. You wait here. Plus, they are two little old ladies. No need to ambush them with all four of us."

"Geez." Dennis winked at me. "Talk about ganging up on a guy. Okay, fine, I'll wait here."

Kade stood, looking down at me. "Coming?"

"Of course!"

We wove our way through the tables, coming to a stop next to the two women. Well, two women and a ghost. Joyce beamed up at me from her seat, her torso protruding through the table since the chair she was sitting on was pushed in.

"Ladies, I believe you are friends with Joyce Harrison?" Kade began, only to be cut off by the woman still wearing her sunglasses.

"Why? What did she do?"

Kade's head jerked from one to the other, but his voice was soft when he said, "I'm sorry to say that she died."

The women's acting skills were atrocious. Over exaggerated gasps of surprise, mouths forming perfect Os, hands clasped against their chests. Kade glanced at me, and I bit my lip to keep from grinning. Yeah, I wasn't buying it either.

"But then I think you already knew that," he continued. "Since the three of you were playing golf together this morning, and we just found her on the green."

They refused to look at us. Instead, they found a sudden and intense interest in the checkered tablecloth, and I knew what the problem was. Kade was a cop, in cop mode, doing cop things. There was no way they were going to open up to him.

I smiled and held out my hand. "I'm Audrey. And this is Kade, and those are his parents at that table over there, Dennis and Sylvia."

"Lovely to meet you. I'm Sally." The woman in the blue shirt shook my hand. "And this is Hazel."

Hazel gave her friend a frustrated look, then plastered a fake smile on her face and begrudgingly shook my hand. "Sorry. This hardly seems the time to be making your acquaintance. You just told us our friend is dead."

"Don't mind her," Joyce said, standing up. "She always acts like she has a stick up her a—"

"I agree," I assured Hazel. "I'm so sorry about your friend. Can you tell us what happened?"

"She just keeled over!" Sally declared, fanning her face.

"Before or after you ran her over?" Kade drawled. Sally paled and looked as if she were about to pass out any second, while Hazel narrowed her eyes and looked at him shrewdly before turning to her friend.

"Don't say another word, Sally."

Kade shot me a look that I couldn't read. Was he mad? Curious? Needed the bathroom? I couldn't tell.

Joyce seemed to be enjoying herself, moving to stand next to me with a giggle. "They're not going to tell you a thing with him towering over them, being all brooding and manly."

"Brooding and manly?" I repeated, only for Sally and Hazel to snap their attention my way.

"Look, we're not man-haters per se. Well, especially not me." Joyce poked me in the ribs with her elbow. "But Hazel here? Not a fan of the male species. And Sally? Well, she'll follow along with whatever the consensus is at any given time, and since I'm out of the equation..."

I got it. They weren't going to open up and tell me anything useful in front of Kade. Especially as he was projecting serious cop vibes. "Babe?" I turned to him and smiled sweetly. "Why don't you go check on your parents?"

"What?" He frowned. "They're fine."

I rolled my eyes but didn't have to say anything because, bless his heart, he put two and two together and said, "Oh! Sure." He walked back to their table, where Sylvia and Dennis were watching us with undisguised interest.

"Okay," I said in a rush, turning back to Hazel and Sally. "He's gone. You have exactly two minutes to tell me what happened here today before he either comes back or the police arrive." It was a bluff. I didn't know if Kade was going to call the police or not.

"Woo-hoo!" Joyce clapped in delight. "I love your style, girl."

"Who are you, exactly?" Hazel said, eyeing me suspiciously.

"I'm Audrey Fitzgerald, private investigator, and I'm your best bet to get the truth of what happened today."

Sally turned to Hazel, her eyes huge behind her glasses. "She's a PI! That's good... isn't it?" She looked from her friend to me and back again. "Oh, wait... that's not good, right? Cos then she'll find out..."

"Sally! Hush!" Hazel snapped.

"Find out what?" I pounced. I was starting to think these two sweet, seventy-something-year-olds may be behind their friend's death after all. They were acting as suspicious as all get out, and the fact that they hadn't called for help after running over their friend was a glaring red flag.

"I told you she was stubborn," Joyce said.

Pulling out my phone, I opened my note app and typed "what is it they don't want me to know?"

"Huh?" Joyce shrugged. "I don't know what you mean."

"The three of you are hiding something. What is it?" I wrote.

Joyce tapped her lip, gazing into the distance before she snapped her fingers and brought her attention back to me. "I think I've got it!"

I looked at her and waited.

"Oh, yes, right." She grinned. "So, you see, Hazel, Sally, and I have a little something going on the side."

"Little something?" I asked, forgetting that Sally and Hazel were sitting right in front of me.

"You know Torres Place has independent living apartments and an aged care facility?"

"I know." I nodded, waving for her to continue.

"Well, some of those residents in the aged care part can feel a little... trapped. Like they're prisoners. And they have all these *rules*!"

"Rules? Like what?"

"No alcohol, no visiting each other's rooms after lights out, no swapping medication with your friends. No fun."

"I hardly think no fun is a rule." And the no swapping medication rule seemed sensible to me.

"Well, it seems like that." Joyce pouted. "It all began when Margaret asked for our help."

"Who's Margaret?"

"She's the eighty-nine-year-old diabetic in room 37C. She asked for chocolate."

"You're telling me you gave a diabetic chocolate?" I had a sinking feeling this didn't end well. For Margaret.

"Of course we did!" Joyce huffed. "She's eighty-nine. What little time she has left should be full of joy, not mired in misery. And we're not stupid. We got her that God-awful sugar-free stuff."

"Who on earth are you talking to?" Hazel interrupted, looking at me as if I had two heads. "Are you, you know"—she tapped her temple— "touched?"

"Touched?" I repeated, not understanding.

"She means are you crazy? Touched in the head. Simple," Joyce gleefully provided.

"Oh! No. I'm not."

"Well, what are you then? Because you are clearly having a conversation with someone other than us."

"Are you talking to Joyce?" Sally asked, clasping her hands together against her chest.

"You may as well tell them. Believe me, these girls can keep a secret."

"I'm starting to see that," I said, then tipped my head back and looked at the ceiling. Chicago was bad for me. Here I was, not one day in and already my secret was outed. Twice!

I leveled my gaze at Hazel and Sally. "Okay, fine, I'll tell you my secret if you tell me yours. I see ghosts. I can communicate with the departed. And yes, your friend Joyce is here with me."

Hazel threw both hands in the air in an I-told-you-so gesture. "There you go then!" she declared. "Just ask her what happened. She'll tell you we didn't kill her."

"I have asked her. She can't remember."

"Really, Joyce?" Hazel rolled her eyes. "Really?"

"Look." I leaned in close, my tone betraying my sense of urgency. "We have a limited amount of time before the authorities arrive. Joyce has already told me you've been supplying chocolate to a diabetic in the care facility at Torres Place. What else do I need to know?"

"Joyce, you snitch!" Hazel grumbled, but her shrewd eyes met mine. "Fine. We help people source the items they require."

"Like what?"

"Oh, you know, things like Viagra for those who—"

I held up my hand, cutting her off. "No need to go into specifics." I did not need the mental imagery of the elderly and Viagra, thank you very much. "Anything illegal?" I pressed. "Anything that could have gotten Joyce killed?"

"What do you mean, got Joyce killed?" Sally whispered, horrified. "She had a heart attack. Didn't she?"

"Look, it's entirely possible Joyce did, in fact, have a heart attack. But, in my experience, when a spirit finds me after they've died, it usually means foul play was involved."

Hazel shook her head. "No. Nothing like that."

Sally chewed her lip, worry plastered all over her face.

"Sally?" I prompted.

Sally shot a look at Hazel, then quickly averted her eyes. "There was that time when we got my grandson to hot-wire Stanley's hearing aids into the nurses' station radio frequency."

"What on earth for?"

"Stanley was a bit of a jerk. He was especially mean to Joyce, called her all sorts of disgusting names. We figured a little retribution was in order," Sally said.

Hazel snorted. "The man thought he was being visited by Jesus."

"He was certainly hearing voices, just not that of our Lord and Savior." Sally chuckled.

Joyce slapped her knee and bent over laughing, "Oh yes, I remember that. We'd sneak into the nurses' station from time to time and whisper to him through the radio."

"And you never got found out?" These three women were wilier than I thought.

"Nope," they said in unison, proud as punch.

I cleared my throat, bringing them back on track. "I want you to think long and hard about anyone who would want to harm Joyce," I told the two women in front of me. "In the meantime, tell me what happened this morning."

Hazel had obviously decided to trust me, for she spoke without hesitation. "We met at the café for breakfast, as per usual. Joyce had scrambled eggs and orange juice. She was fine until she wasn't. She went all pasty looking, clutched at her chest, then slumped back in her chair. Dead."

I blinked in shock. "You're saying Joyce died at the café?"

"Yes." Sally nodded, clutching her friend's arm.

"Let me get this straight. She died at the café after eating breakfast?"

They nodded.

"And then you...?"

"We put her in the golf cart and brought her out onto the course," Sally said.

"For all that is holy, why? Why move her?"

"Because we thought, if you have to go out, it's better to go out on a golf course than here. Joyce loved it out there, and we wanted her death to be more... fitting," Hazel said.

"But then she fell out of the cart," Sally added.

"We didn't strap her in." Hazel had the grace to look apologetic. "I wasn't expecting her to be so floppy. The slightest turn and she slid right out of the buggy, and before I knew it, I'd run her over."

"Ha ha ha." Joyce barked out a laugh in my ear. "That's priceless. They wanted everyone to think I'd died playing golf. Aw, these two are the best friends ever."

"Why did you leave her? After she fell out of the buggy?"

"I panicked. It wasn't my finest moment," Hazel confessed. "I was trying to get her back in the cart when we saw you coming. We abandoned our plan and ran."

Sally reached across the table and patted her friend's hand while saying to Joyce, "No offense, Joyce, but as a dead person, you are heavy. And slippery."

"None taken," Joyce replied, beaming at Sally. I had to say, she was taking all of this rather well. I, on the other hand, felt like I'd walked into a seventies sit-com.

CHAPTER FIVE

"So you see, being run over by a golf buggy didn't kill her. She was already dead." I finished telling the others what had transpired between Sally, Hazel, and Joyce that morning.

"How did no one notice?" Sylvia murmured, eyes wide. "How did no-one notice two old ladies dragging a dead body out of here?"

"I guess everyone is busy with their own business," I suggested, but honestly, I didn't have an answer for her. Sally and Hazel had supported their friend between them as they left the terrace because Joyce had been in a sitting position to begin with. Easy enough to wrap her arms around their shoulders, slide their arms around her waist and basically drag her to the golf cart. But when she fell out of the buggy, trying to get her off the ground? That was a different story entirely. And then we'd appeared on the horizon, and they'd panicked, leaving their friend behind.

"I think it's sweet," Sylvia said, eyes misty. "But also sad."

"Sweet?" Dennis barked. "They interfered with a corpse!"

The way he said it made it sound gross and oh, so wrong. Cringey even.

"They were trying to honor their friend," Sylvia argued. "They weren't doing anything malicious."

"Regardless," I cut in, "Joyce's ghost found me. Which makes me believe she didn't die of natural causes. And her friends didn't kill her. So the question remains, who killed her, and how?"

Dennis pulled out his phone, mumbling beneath his breath as he scrolled through his contacts. "I have friends on the force. I can get them to expedite Joyce's autopsy."

"Would they even do an autopsy, given her age?" Kade said.

"I can plant the seed of doubt, say that she was run over—they can't dispute that. Any fool could see the tire marks on her body—so the facility, not to mention her family, need a definite cause of death."

Whoever Dennis was calling picked up, and while Dennis was chatting with his buddy, I leaned over to Kade. "Can he really do that?"

Kade shrugged. "I don't know if he has that much pull, but it doesn't hurt to put a little pressure on the coroner's department, to let them know someone is looking into Joyce's death, make them aware they can't rubber stamp it."

"Rubber stamp?"

"Mark it off as natural causes, or even a heart attack, without doing an autopsy."

My phone started buzzing and a quick glance at the screen showed a video call from Seb. Seb was my extremely hot, extremely gay neighbor, who was pet sitting Thor, my overweight-and-currently-on-a-diet British shorthair cat, and Bandit, my adopted raccoon.

Answering the call, I stood, hurrying out of the café so as not to disturb anyone.

"Seb!" I beamed at the screen. "How's it going? Is everything okay?"

"Good morning, sunshine. How goes Chicago?" Seb beamed at me, his white teeth dazzling as usual.

"Let me see, let me see." Bandit came into shot

for the briefest of moments, pushed aside by Thor, whose big gray teddy bear head filled the screen.

"When are you coming home?" he meowed. "I'm dying here. Seb is trying to starve me to death!"

I snorted out a laugh. Thor was on a diet, as per the vet's instructions, and to say he was being dramatic about it was an understatement.

"I've only been gone a few hours," I soothed. "You're not starving and you're certainly not dying."

"Mom! Mom! Mom!" Bandit was back, climbing onto Thor's back and pressing her nose to the screen. All I could see was nostrils.

"Hey, Bandit, miss you," I cooed, and I swear she practically swooned, flopping over and rubbing her snout all over Seb's phone.

"They're fine," Seb half shouted over the ruckus. "We're doing fine. I don't know what Thor told you, but he is not starving, and there is kibble in his bowl."

"Lies! It's all lies!" Thor bellowed.

"No, Thor, look." Bandit grabbed Thor's head with both paws and twisted so he was facing the food dishes near the back door. For a second, I was worried she'd wrench his head clean off. "There's kibble."

"Oh!" Thor brightened, jumped down from the

kitchen counter, and padded over to the food bowl. "So there is."

"You know they're not meant to be on the counter, Seb," I said, once the pair had decided they weren't in mortal peril and starvation wasn't imminent.

"I figured we could make an exception while I called you." Seb waved away my concern, but what he didn't realize was now that they had the okay, they figured it was forever. From here on out, I was going to have a battle to keep them off the counter, and Kade had a thing about pets not being allowed on food preparation surfaces. I figured he got to have that rule since he did most of the cooking.

"Plus, you've got other fish to worry about," Seb continued. He propped the phone against something on the bench-top and was using his hands as he talked. "None other than para-legal extraordinaire, the one and only Amanda Fitzgerald, has not only called me twice already today, she has actually dropped in, gracing me with her presence."

"Amanda dropped in? Why?" Amanda was my sister-in-law, married to my brother Dustin, and they had two adorable kids, Madeline and Nathaniel. Amanda was drop-dead gorgeous, smart, and a pain in my butt. She was forever trying to *fix* my clumsy trait. I knew her constant interference was based on good intentions but lordy, she could be *a lot*.

"You're not going to like it," Seb said dramatically.

"Just tell me."

"She wants your wedding album."

I frowned, confused. "My wedding album? I'm not married yet. I don't have an album."

"No, not a photography album. A planner. The scrapbook planner women make when planning out their dream wedding."

I blinked, shocked. "That's a thing?"

Seb giggled. "I knew you wouldn't have one. That's what I told Amanda. It's like she doesn't even know you. You are the least girly girl I know. To imagine you've been planning your wedding since you were a little girl is ludicrous. No offense."

"None taken. It's perfectly true. But even if I had one of these wedding planning albums things, what does she want it for?"

Seb heaved a heartfelt sigh and air quoted, "She has concerns."

I groaned, and a pit formed in my stomach. It was stressful enough getting married without having to contend with Amanda's interference. Which was why I'd hired Seb to be my wedding planner. He was much better at this stuff than I was, and I was grateful to have him, not only as a neighbor but as a friend.

"I bet she does," I grumbled. "What is it this time? She doesn't think I should wear a veil because I'd probably set it on fire? I can't wear a white dress because I'll spill wine on it? I shouldn't wear my hair up because my face is too round?"

Seb guffawed, almost doubling over while he laughed. "All the above," he chortled, clearly very amused, but then he sobered. "She says that she thinks it's in your best interests that she should have the final say."

"The final say on what?" I mean, it wasn't going to happen, but I was curious what Amanda wanted control of.

"Everything!" Seb swept his arms wide. "The dress, the cake, the venue, the decorations, the photographer, the officiant."

"But you're the officiant," I pointed out. "It's already arranged."

"We"—he pointed from me to him—"both know that, but Amanda is struggling to accept that you're not getting married in a church with a priest officiating."

I shrugged. "That's just too bad. Look, ignore

everything she says. She doesn't get a say in this at all."

"Sugar, I know that," Seb assured me. "Just wanted to let you know that as soon as the cat's away, the mouse comes over and starts interfering."

I pinched the bridge of my nose. "Sorry she's doing this." I knew how annoying my sister-in-law could be, and the worst part was, she wasn't like this to be mean or horrible. It came from a place of love, and I fully understood that. But that wasn't to say I liked it.

"Hey," Seb protested, leaning forward, his face filling the screen, "I didn't tell you to bring you down. I just wanted you to know, is all. I've got this. If I can handle drag queens with missing lashes, I can handle the likes of Amanda with one hand tied behind my back and a martini in the other."

Then Seb shivered and pulled back from his phone. "I think Ben's here. I can feel him."

Ben was the ghost of my best friend. He'd been the start of my crazy journey of becoming a PI when, with his ghostly help, I'd solved his murder. I'd also inherited his house, business, and cat, Thor. The whole being able to talk to and understand animals thing had been another curve ball that I'd had to come to terms with, and even though I didn't fully understand how it had all come about, Ben and I thought it had something to do with his previous neighbor's predilection for witchcraft.

"Ben?" I looked over Seb's shoulder but couldn't see him. "Ben?" I tried again. Nothing. I sighed. I wished I hadn't told him to stay home now. He could help me with Joyce.

"No?" Seb interrupted my thoughts. "You can't see him? I'm sure he's here. My skin is all ring-a-ting-tingly."

I shook my head. "Nope. Maybe he is there, but because I'm not, I've lost the connection."

Before I could say anything more, the screen filled with static. "Seb?" I shook my phone, then almost dropped it when Ben's voice came through the speaker. "Really, Fitz? You think shaking it will fix the problem?"

"Ben!" I smiled, happy to hear his voice. His face swam into view, but he was distorted, fuzzy, and pixelated. "I can barely see you."

"Yeah, that's because I'm in Seb's phone. So, how's Chicago? And more importantly, how did it go with the parentals?"

"Oh God, Ben, you wouldn't believe it! Within minutes of meeting them, a ghost turns up, only I didn't realize she was a ghost. I thought she was a friend or relative of the Galloways, and here's me, openly chatting with thin air!"

"How did they take it?"

"Surprisingly well," I admitted with a rueful grin. "Sylvia Galloway is into the alternative stuff, crystals and horoscopes and what not, and of course Dennis is a retired cop, so he was all 'how did this person die? We need to investigate,' and before I know it, all four of us are in search of Joyce's body."

Ben froze. "Are you telling me, Audrey Fitzgerald, that on your trip to Chicago to meet your fiancé's parents for the first time, you are now involved in a murder investigation?"

"Is that bad?" I whispered. When he put it that way, it sounded bad.

"Well, I guess as long as you're bonding with your future in-laws, what does it matter how you go about it?"

"Really?" I asked hopefully. I'd been in knots about meeting them, had been mortified I'd been caught talking to a ghost, but solving the mystery behind Joyce's death *was* a bonding experience.

"Audrey... what's up? Since when have you needed my approval on anything you do?" Ben was nothing if not perceptive. Probably because we'd grown up next door to each other. He'd been my best friend my entire life. And now his afterlife.

"Nothing, it's fine." I shook my head, then blurted, "It's just the whole wedding stuff. Amanda has been bothering Seb, demanding she get the final say in my arrangements. Our arrangements," I hastily corrected, for the wedding wasn't just about me. It was Kade's special day, too.

"You're worrying about Amanda?" The way he said it made it sound like I had rocks in my head. He confirmed that by saying, "Have you got rocks in your head? Of all the things, her antics are what's bothering you the most? Fitz, get a grip. Seb has this handled—except for the part about telling you. He should have kept it to himself cos now you're obsessing over it—but other than that, you know he has your back. He won't let her derail anything. Just relax, enjoy your time in Chicago, get to know your out-laws. Solve a murder if you must, but quit worrying about what's happening back here in Firefly Bay. That's an order."

"Yes, sir!" I giggled. I didn't realize how much I needed to hear that until Ben basically told me to pull my head out of my butt and quit worrying. "Well, I guess I should get back. We have a murder to solve, after all."

CHAPTER SIX

"Everything okay?" Kade asked when I returned.

Sliding back into my seat, I nodded. "The usual. Thor thinks he's being starved, Bandit misses us, and Seb is running interference on the wedding front."

Kade's eyes narrowed, not missing my tone when I mentioned the wedding. "What's happened?"

"Nothing. Nothing for you to worry about. Now, where are we with our investigation?" I plastered a smile on my face and ignored the look that passed between Kade and his mother. I was fine. Everything was fine.

When the group remained silent, I felt a growing urge to steer the conversation in a different direction, away from our upcoming wedding.

"So, Joyce mentioned something interesting earlier," I began, eager to shift the focus. "Apparently, she and the ladies have a side hustle going on."

Dennis leaned forward, his curiosity piqued. "Side hustle?" he asked, his eyes lighting up.

I paused for a moment, gathering my thoughts. "Well, they've been doing all sorts of things, really," I explained. "Mainly, they've been helping the residents in the aged care section of the facility. But I have a feeling there's more to it than that."

"You think one of these activities could have gotten Joyce killed?" Kade asked, eyebrows askance. I know it sounded like a long shot, but my mind kept drifting back to what Joyce had told me earlier, about Margaret the diabetic and her desire for chocolate. If residents were swapping medication and something had gone horribly wrong, it wouldn't be a stretch to imagine someone thought Joyce, Hazel, and Sally were responsible.

Before I could answer, Dennis downed the rest of his coffee and slammed his cup down on the table. "Right, let's get this show on the road!" He made a move to stand, but I held up a hand, signaling him to halt.

"Hold on," I urged. "Not so fast. We need to

divide and conquer. Hazel doesn't like men. She's more likely to open up and cooperate with me and Sylvia than you two."

"What do you suggest?" Kade asked.

I tapped my lip for a moment, eyeing Dennis. Now that he'd had a moment to rest, he looked better, certainly sounded much more chipper. "Dennis, earlier when we met the chief operations managers, you and he got into a little discussion about how deaths are handled at Torres Place. Can you dig into that? Find out if there have been other suspicious deaths?" I turned to Kade. "I thought you and your dad could pursue that angle while Sylvia and I go talk to the ladies."

Dennis and Sylvia exchanged a look, then Dennis turned his attention back to me and opened his mouth to speak, but Kade beat him to it.

"Sure. I wouldn't mind spending some quality father and son time. How about you, Dad?"

"Oh, well—" Dennis blustered, his cheeks taking on a ruddy hue. Clearing his throat, he said, "Yes, that sounds fine."

This was where I missed Ben. Ben would have noticed that strange exchange and told me what he thought it was all about. As it was, I had no clue, but there was no time to worry about it now. Over

Dennis's shoulder, I saw Hazel and Sally preparing to leave the café.

"Come on," I said to Sylvia. "They're making a move. I don't want to lose them."

"Oh, right!" Sylvia hurriedly finished her drink, dabbed at her mouth with a napkin, and gave her husband a quick peck on the cheek before following me as I hurried after Hazel and Sally. I thought I heard Dennis say, "Is she always like that?" but couldn't be sure. Maybe I was projecting. Maybe I was interpreting the look he'd shared with his wife all wrong.

As we rounded the corner, Hazel and Sally came into view, chatting by the elevator doors that led to the east wing. I quickened my pace, eager to catch up with them.

"Ladies," I called out as we approached. "We need to talk."

Joyce, who was with her friends, turned to greet us, a smile spreading across her face. "Oh, hey," she said. "You're here. That's great. It'll give you a chance to get to know Hazel and Sally better. They're not bad people. They're very dear friends who were trying to do right by me."

I nodded in understanding but made no reply as we all stepped into the elevator. Hazel hit the button for the sixth floor, casting me a sly look. "We didn't kill Joyce, you know," she said, crossing her arms. "Why would we? She was our friend. And you don't even know if she was murdered. You're just guessing. I still think she had a heart attack." Hazel had clearly had time to think things over.

"Did she have heart issues?" Sylvia asked. "Sorry, we haven't been properly introduced. I'm Sylvia Galloway. My husband, Dennis, and I moved into Torres Place a little while ago."

"I'm Sally." Sally raised her hand in a wave. "This is Hazel. How are you settling in? I know when I first moved here, it was so different, so strange, but then I had been living with my daughter and her family and, well, things were squeezy to put it mildly, but then of course Meghan gets pregnant—again—and they needed my room for the baby, so I had to be re-homed."

I blinked in surprise. Re-homed? Sally made it sound like she was a discarded pet.

"Actually, we're loving it here. Before this, we were traveling around Australia in an RV, so after living in a motor home for longer than I'd care to admit, apartment living is luxurious," Sylvia said.

"Sally," Hazel hissed, nudging her friend in the

ribs. "This isn't a social call. They're here to ask about Joyce."

Sally frowned. "What about her?" She sounded genuinely puzzled, and I wondered if Sally had a touch of dementia.

Hazel rolled her eyes. "They think we killed her. Am I right, ladies?"

"Actually, I don't think that at all," I said, somewhat smugly. "Honestly, we don't know if Joyce was killed or if she died of natural causes. There really is no evidence to suggest foul play, except for the fact that her ghost is here. I've never had a ghost turn up when a person has simply died. They only come to me if they were murdered."

"You know you sound insane, right?" Hazel looked down her nose at me, and I shrugged. I was taking a chance. Joyce had vouched for her friends, and I'd been doing this long enough to know that, despite not wanting to believe ghosts existed, Hazel believed me. I also thought Hazel was mortified about what had happened to Joyce, how their big grand gesture of taking her out on the golf course for one last round had gone horrendously wrong, and now she was full of bluff and bluster while simultaneously trying to deal with her emotions. I got it. I felt like that on the daily.

"Let's go with the theory that Joyce was killed by a person or persons unknown." I ignored her dig. "Who did you see this morning? Who did Joyce interact with?"

"And is there anyone she has a beef with?" Sylvia chimed in. "With this buy, swap, sell venture y'all have going on, did something happen with that? Did Joyce upset someone? Hurt someone—unintentionally, of course."

Sally frowned. "Joyce would never hurt anyone!"

"Unintentionally, Sally." Hazel turned to her friend. "It means not on purpose."

"I know what it means." Sally sniffed, pouting.

The elevator dinged, and the doors slid open. "You may as well come to my place," Hazel less than graciously invited as she stepped out of the elevator. "I have snacks."

"Hey, I have snacks too," Sally protested, following her out.

"Yes, but your snacks are inedible." Hazel didn't look back, and Sylvia and I trotted along behind her, listening as the two women bickered over Sally's snacks. Apparently, she baked them herself, and it sounded like Sally's baking skills were on par with mine. Nonexistent.

"Hazel's right," Joyce said in my ear. "You

wouldn't feed Sally's snacks to your dog. But bless her, she keeps on trying. And trying. And trying. If anything was going to kill me, it'd be one of her snacks."

I stopped walking, Hazel, Sally, and Sylvia not noticing I'd fallen behind. "Of course," I whispered, turning to look at Joyce, who'd stopped with me. "You had to have been poisoned. I hadn't really thought about how you were killed, but poison makes perfect sense. You weren't stabbed, shot, or strangled. This was a murder of opportunity. Someone slipped something to you."

"Audrey?" Sylvia called my name. She was standing in the open doorway of what I assumed was Hazel's apartment, the others no longer in sight. "Everything okay?"

"Coming."

"It wasn't Sally." Joyce grabbed my arm as I hurried to catch up. "I don't eat her snacks. On account of they could kill you. Unless I committed suicide? Oh my gosh, I didn't, did I?"

I shot her a look. "No, Joyce, I do not believe you took your own life. And I don't think Sally killed you either. Or Hazel. If either of your friends were behind this, they'd have left you in the café, not taken you out on the golf course for one last hurrah."

"Oh, good. Right. Let's go catch my killer, then."

"Everything okay?" Sylvia asked, ushering me inside Hazel's apartment.

"Just having a quick word with Joyce." My mouth stretched into a tight smile, not reaching my eyes. It felt all kinds of weird talking with Kade's mom about my ghost chatting abilities. My mom didn't even know, and weirdly, this felt like a betrayal, though I didn't fully understand why I felt that way.

Hazel's apartment was straight out of the seventies. Or maybe it was the eighties, but either way, it was *something*. Cane furniture with palm tree cushions, matching palm curtains, and a green shag rug in front of the tan sofa. Requisite recliner in the prime television viewing spot.

"Wow," I whispered. The layout was similar to the Galloways' apartment. Open plan. A small kitchen area was dominated by an olive-green counter and mustard tiled backsplash with decorative sunflower tiles dispersed throughout, a dining area with a round, glass-topped table on a cane pedestal, and straw placemats in front of each chair. The view was different. While the Galloways' apartment faced Lake Michigan, Hazel's faced the museum across the street.

"Oh I love it," Sylvia cooed. "Very Florida-esqe."

"It was like this when I bought it," Hazel dead-panned. "Never got around to decorating."

"Ha!" Joyce barked, making me jump. "Don't let her fool you. She loves the decor. Even that darn palm tree wallpaper. I mean, if this place was mine, I'd strip everything out and start over. Hazel claims she doesn't have the funds, but I know she has a very healthy bank balance. She just doesn't like to spend money."

"Where's Joyce's apartment?" I asked. "Does she live nearby?"

"She's next door. I'm in the middle. Sally is on the other side."

"Oh, you're neighbors. Is that how you met?" Sylvia asked, making herself comfortable on the sofa.

"Joyce and I moved in at the same time and quickly became friends," Sally said, sitting next to Sylvia. "Hazel moved in a couple of years later."

"They dragged me into their friendship, whether I wanted it or not," Hazel said drolly.

"And it was the best thing that ever happened to her," Joyce added. "She was lonely until she met us."

"Do you have a key? I'd like to look around."

"You think there's a clue in my apartment?" Joyce asked.

"Why?" Hazel narrowed her eyes, her spine stiffening.

I sighed and shook my head. "Look, I'm not going to take anything. I have a theory."

"Let's hear it." Hazel beckoned me to continue. She was a tough cookie to crack, that was for sure.

"I think Joyce may have been poisoned."

Sally gasped, clapping her hands to her cheeks. "And you think the poison is in Joyce's apartment?"

Hazel rolled her eyes and heaved a heartfelt sigh. "No, Sally. Obviously, the killer isn't going to leave a big bottle of poison out for us to find. No, I think what Audrey is saying is that the killer may have poisoned something in Joyce's apartment. Something she ate or drank."

"Or came into contact with in some way," I added.

"Assuming she was poisoned," Sylvia pointed out.

"Assuming that," I agreed. It was just a theory. "If Dennis's friend can get the ME's office to put a rush on a toxicology report, then we'll know for sure."

CHAPTER SEVEN

"Joyce," I hissed, holding a screwed up note in my hand. "Why didn't you tell me about this?"

"It's nothing," she dismissed with a wave of her hand, instead intent on running her fingers over the furniture in her apartment, which was a stark contrast to Hazel's. Instead of palm print and shades of green and orange, Joyce's décor was soft white, natural fibers, very earthy. I liked it.

Hazel had begrudgingly agreed that it wasn't a terrible idea to search Joyce's apartment for anything toxic, and here we were, all of us digging through her belongings. I'd been worried Joyce may protest at the invasion of privacy, but she appeared to be enthralled with attempting to touch and pick up various objects, which, of course, she couldn't because she was a ghost.

"What is it?" Sylvia asked, rushing to my side. She'd been pulling books from Joyce's bookcase and shaking them to see if anything fell out. I hadn't had the heart to tell her I highly doubted the books were the source of poison.

"It's a letter from Jay Perry threatening legal action," I said. I'd found it screwed up in the wastepaper basket next to the narrow dresser in Joyce's dining area.

"What?" Hazel stormed over and snatched the crumpled letter from my hand, silently scanning the contents. Flabbergasted, she raised her head, hand dropping to her side, the letter fluttering from her fingers to fall silently on the carpet. "She never said a word."

"I didn't want to worry you," Joyce said.

"She didn't want to worry you," I automatically passed on the message.

"Plus, it never eventuated. Jay cooled down, and nothing ever came of it."

"He accused you of killing his mother. Please tell me his mother isn't called Margaret, the diabetic you bought chocolate for," I said.

"It was *sugar-free*," she stressed, then rolled her shoulders. "And as a matter of fact, yes. Yes, his mother was Margaret, the diabetic *we* bought the chocolate for." She pointed to Hazel and Sally.

"What's she saying?" Hazel demanded, eyes narrowed into mere slits.

"She said that Jay cooled off and this"—I reached down and picked up the letter—"all went away. That Jay's mother was Margaret. She was a diabetic, and you bought her chocolate."

"Sugar free," Hazel and Sally said simultaneously.

My chin slumped to my chest as I thought about the ramifications this presented. These women had purchased chocolate for a known diabetic who had subsequently died. Her son had obviously caught wind of it and threatened to sue. "How did he know you were involved?" I asked Joyce. Because the letter was addressed to her and her alone.

She shrugged. "I told him, of course. After Margaret passed. I went to check in on her only they stopped me at her door, said she'd passed, and then he—Jay—came to the door asking if I knew his mother, if we were friends. I told him we were, and that I bought her chocolate and I hoped she enjoyed it, you know, a last little piece of happiness before crossing through the pearly gates."

"What's she saying?" Hazel asked.

"She said she told Jay that she bought his mother the chocolate."

"Joyce!" Hazel threw her hands in the air. "How many times must I tell you? What we do is a *secret!*"

Joyce cringed. "Sorry."

"She says she's sorry," I dutifully repeated. "Why is it a secret?"

"Because some people give us money," Sally piped up.

Hazel swung on her heel and glared at her friend. "Hush your mouth," she hissed.

"Okay, okay." I waved the women to shush. "Ladies, I need you to be straight with me. We think your friend was *murdered*. This is no time to be keeping secrets. I can't stress how important it is that you tell me what's been going on. Who paid you money and what for?"

Hazel clamped her lips shut and crossed her arms, the epitome of stubbornness. Sally crumpled like a tower of cards in the slightest breeze.

"There's a red hot market in Viagra for the men, and Valium for the women," Sally said. "We've built up quite a network of... sources."

"What she's getting at," Joyce continued, "is that people who have a prescription for such things but no longer require them allow us to buy the medications from them, and we then resell them to anyone who has the need."

"Oh my God! You're drug dealers?" I mean, I shouldn't have been surprised, but seriously, who would have thought it? These three women in their seventies peddling Viagra and Valium?

Hazel and Sally exchanged a look but didn't say a word. Sylvia, who had been listening with rapt attention, finally blurted, "How entrepreneurial. Don't you think so, Audrey?"

"That's one word for it," I said. "So, what happened?"

"Nothing," Hazel barked. "Absolutely nothing happened. It's business as usual."

"No one died? No one became ill? You didn't get found out?"

"Nope." This time, all three replied.

I began pacing as I digested this latest piece of news. Joyce had received a threatening letter regarding Margaret's death, but that hadn't been drug related, it had been chocolate related. I stopped mid-stride. "Joyce, you didn't sell Margaret drugs, did you?"

"Actually, she was one of the ones we bought them from. Valium. The doctors put her on them a couple of years ago, but she said she didn't like taking them. They made her feel all fuzzy and woozy, and she couldn't think straight, so she'd pretend to take them and then stash them in her bedside table. We offered to take them off her hands."

"You were exchanging Valium for chocolate?" My eyes must have been out on stalks.

"Sugar free."

"What's she saying?" Sylvia grabbed my arm, keen to know more.

"She's saying that Margaret was one of their suppliers." I eyed Hazel and Sally. "Ladies, this has to stop. It's dangerous. Medications like this need to be monitored, and you're giving them out willy-nilly. It's a miracle you haven't killed anyone!"

"But—" Sally began, but I cut her off.

"This stops. Now. You can either put an end to it, or I'll call the authorities, and there'll be ramifications you may not like." I really didn't want to have to rat them out, but I would if pushed. What they were doing was foolhardy and dangerous.

Hazel clamped her lips together, her tongue

running over her teeth as she glared at me. She knew I was right, but she was having a darned hard time admitting it.

"Hazel?" I pushed. "Are we in agreement? The drug dealing has got to stop."

Her lips thinned so much they disappeared. "Fine."

"Hand over your stash. And don't tell me you don't have one." These little old ladies had set themselves up a nice supply and demand side gig, and to meet demand, they had to have the supply. Sally was looking at Hazel with wide eyes, chewing her lip. I didn't think Sally had the stash. She was too easy to crack. Which left Hazel or Joyce.

"Joyce? Do you keep them here?"

Joyce had drifted over to the kitchen, trying to open the refrigerator. "What's that, love?" she asked absently, then shook her head. "Nope. Hazel keeps inventory. I do deliveries."

"And what does Sally do?"

"Oh, she looks after the money." Joyce shrugged. "Sally gets confused real easy. Gave Donald Valium instead of Viagra that one time and the poor man fell asleep on top of his date. On the upside, he slept a solid twelve hours and declared he'd never slept better. Sally is ditzy, but she has a head for numbers."

"Let me get this straight," I said to the room. "Hazel is in control of inventory, Joyce is distribution, and Sally handles the cash. Correct?"

Sally nodded, and Hazel slapped her arm.

"Ow!" Sally wailed. "What did you do that for?"

"Stop telling her everything!" Hazel wailed.

"I'm not!" Sally protested. "Joyce is. Or maybe Audrey is just smart and worked it out for herself."

"Ladies, ladies, ladies." Sylvia muscled her way between the two arguing women. "Calm down. The truth of the matter is that what you were doing is illegal. Count yourselves lucky it's Audrey and me here and not my son, who is a bona fide police detective. He'd have no option but to arrest you. And we don't want that. Do we, Audrey?"

"No, we don't. We're here to find out what happened to Joyce."

"And it seems to me that it's highly likely her death is related to this little drug operation you have going on. So, it'll behoove you to tell the truth and let us help you," Sylvia finished.

"See?" Sally harrumphed. "Sometimes, Hazel, you have to let people help you."

"Hazel has trust issues." Joyce gave up trying to

open the refrigerator. "Mostly because of the three ex-husbands. All of them losers." She turned to her friend. "Come on, Hazel, go get the stash. We had a good run while it lasted, but the jig is up."

"Joyce says you should go get the stash," I said. "She says the jig is up."

"Fine!" Hazel threw her hands in the air and spun away. "Come on, then."

"Sylvia, are you okay to take care of this? I want to finish searching Joyce's apartment."

She looked shocked. "Oh. Okay, sure. Erm, what do I do with the drugs?"

"Take them back to your apartment. Discretely. We'll work out what to do with them from there." I didn't want to say in front of the others that I fully intended to tell Kade and his father what these women had been up to. But first, we needed to get the drugs out of their hands and appropriately disposed of.

After the three of them had left, I got to work searching Joyce's apartment in earnest. Having my future mother-in-law, Sally, and Hazel help had been more of a hindrance than anything, but now that I had the place to myself, I could get it over with much faster.

"If Joyce was poisoned," I said to myself, "the

easiest way would be to put something in her food or drink." I headed to the kitchen, pulled open the refrigerator, and began sniffing everything that had been opened. "But she didn't have breakfast here," I whispered, putting the milk back in the door. "What was your morning routine, Joyce?"

Only Joyce wasn't there. She'd gone with the others, leaving me to figure this out for myself. "Okay, Audrey. You've got this. If you were Joyce, what's the first thing you'd do when you got up in the morning?"

Pee. Abandoning the fridge, I headed for the bathroom. The vanity was covered with cosmetics and skin care products. Had one of them been tampered with? Maybe the poison hadn't been ingested but was topical? It'd be so much easier if I knew what, exactly, I was searching for. Opening jars and unscrewing lids, I sniffed. Impossible to tell if anything dangerous had been added over the perfumed scent of her creams and lotions, and I wasn't so stupid that I'd try out the creams and accidentally poison myself.

The sound of a key in the lock followed by the front door opening had me freezing in my tracks. Someone was there, and I was about to get busted snooping. Horrified, I glanced around for a place to hide. Slim pickings in the bathroom. Heart hammering in my chest, I slid behind the door and hoped whoever was there did not need to use the bathroom.

Holding my breath, I listened. I could faintly make out muffled footsteps as whoever had entered Joyce's apartment moved around. Burning with curiosity, I daren't stick my head out in case I got caught. Who was out there? Her family? I hadn't asked Joyce about her family, but I'd seen framed photographs around her apartment of Joyce and a younger version of herself—her daughter, I assumed. Maybe her daughter was here?

The footsteps moved closer. They were in the bedroom now, and with the bathroom door ajar, I took a risk and peeked. It was not Joyce's daughter. It was a man. A man wearing a navy suit. I watched as he rummaged through Joyce's bedside table. He cursed, slamming the drawer closed, and as he simultaneously turned and straightened, I caught sight of his face. Paul Wilson was searching through Joyce's belongings!

I must have gasped out loud, for he pivoted my way, and I clamped a hand over my mouth and plastered my back to the wall. Sucking in my belly, I tried to become one with the plasterboard. His footsteps crossed to the bathroom, and I squeezed my eyes shut. He'd seen me. I froze, thinking I'd been caught red-handed. But to my surprise, he didn't yank the door open and drag me out by the hair.

Instead, he searched the vanity, opening and closing drawers and cupboard doors. "Where did you put it, you interfering old bi—" His phone rang, and I almost jumped out of my skin.

"Wilson," he barked. "Yeah, okay. I'm in the laundry. Tell him I'll be there in ten." Hanging up, he cursed up a storm, the words leaving his mouth so foul I had to say, I was taken aback. I mean, I knew a few swear words myself, but Paul Wilson was expanding my vocabulary in a way I didn't know was possible.

He stormed out of the bathroom, shoving the door as he passed. It bounced off my nose. I did my best to hold in the garbled groan as pain exploded across my face, hoping he'd think the door had ricocheted off the wall and not someone hiding behind it. It was a whole new level of torture. Every breath felt like I was inhaling fire, and every movement had my eyes streaming like a broken faucet.

I needn't have worried. He didn't notice at all, didn't pause, didn't hesitate. The apartment door slammed, and slowly, I eased out of my hiding spot, blood dripping onto my shirt as my heartbeat pulsed through my no-doubt fractured nose.

CHAPTER EIGHT

"What happened to your face?"

It was a fair question considering I'd returned to the Galloways' apartment with a wad of tissue shoved up each nostril and bloodstains on my shirt. My face *throbbed*. It throbbed with my heartbeat; it throbbed with every step I took. It just throbbed. I'd never appreciated what throbbing really meant before, but now I did. Zero stars. Do not recommend.

"Do you think it's broken?" I looked up at Kade, who was staring at me incredulously as he held open the door for me to enter.

"Uh, yeah!" He nodded vigorously, then gathered himself, taking my arm and guiding me into the apartment. "Are you okay? What happened?"

Hearing the concern in her son's voice, Sylvia joined us in the narrow entryway.

She gasped. "What happened to your face?"

"Door," I replied.

"Door?" they echoed.

"I got hit in the face with a door." I shrugged. "Now, if you don't mind, I'd like to get cleaned up."

"Babe, I think you need to see a doctor." Kade, having gotten over his initial shock, was all concern.

"I think if I showed up at a doctor's office looking like this, I'd frighten the patients," I joked. "Let me get cleaned up and assess the damage." I was trying to be brave in front of Sylvia. "Sweetheart, could you grab me a fresh shirt out of my bag?"

Kade ignored me. "Mom, do you have any Tylenol? Advil?"

"Of course!" Sylvia hurried away while Kade followed me into the bathroom, standing behind me while I surveyed myself in the mirror. Oh boy, that door hit me like a wrecking ball, leaving me with a nose that looked like it had taken a right hook from Mike Tyson. It was swollen, and dark bruises were forming under my eyes. If I sneezed, it would be a confetti cannon of blood and snot. Best not to sneeze.

"It's fine. Look, it's still straight. I don't think it's broken." I wasn't about to poke it to find out, though.

"Audrey," Kade growled, frustration emanating from him in waves. "You need medical attention."

I spun around and reached up, cupping his face in my palms. "Babe." I tried to make my voice as reassuring as possible, which was harder than anticipated because of the mouth breathing situation I had going on. "You're forgetting that this is normal for me. I'm the clumsiest person you know, remember? Bumps and bruises are par for the course." I choked out a laugh. "Par for the course! Get it? A golf pun."

"Oh har, har. Excuse me for not laughing while you stand here bleeding with a broken nose you refuse to acknowledge," he grumbled.

I dropped my hands and stared at him. "What's with the tone?"

"What tone?"

"That tone! That pissy tone. The one with attitude. Do you think I did *this* on purpose?" I pointed to my face, my ire rising to match his. I didn't get why he was mad at me. Heck, I was always bumping into things, falling over, injuring myself in some form or another. It should come as no surprise to learn a door had hit me in the face.

He stared at me for a second longer before shaking his head. "Sorry. You're right, there was a tone."

"Are *you* okay?" I turned back to the mirror and watched his reflection as he rested his hands on my shoulders, his face etched with worry lines. He had been like this since we arrived, ever since he'd seen for himself how his father's health had taken a turn for the worse.

"Kade, are you okay?" I repeated, putting a hand over his where it rested on my shoulder. I felt bad that I was adding to his worries.

He met my gaze in the mirror, and I saw the pain and concern in his eyes. "I hadn't realized how bad Dad's leg is. He's in constant pain. I'm just worried, you know?"

I nodded, feeling a lump form in my throat. Kade's father had always been a strong and independent man, but now he couldn't walk without a cane, and mobility was clearly an issue. I could only imagine how hard it was for Kade to see his father like this.

"Is there anything I can do to help?" I asked.

Kade shook his head. "No, it's okay. It was just a shock. Mom warned me that his leg was giving him trouble, that he needed to slow down, and they were adjusting their lifestyle because of it. I thought I was prepared."

I turned and wrapped my arms around him, feeling his body tense up before he relaxed into my embrace. "He'll be fine. He's tough," I whispered.

Kade pulled away, wiping a smear of blood from my cheek. "Yeah, I know. Thanks, Audrey. I don't know what I'd do without you."

I gave him a reassuring smile. "You don't have to do anything alone. I'm here for you, always."

Kade nodded, the twinkle returning to his eyes. "I know. And I'm grateful for that. Now"—he leaned down and dropped a kiss on my forehead—"to ease my worried mind, how about we get you checked out by a medical professional, hmmm?"

I narrowed my eyes, a movement which hurt more than I cared to admit. "Was this a ploy? To trick me into seeing a doctor?"

He feigned a hurt expression before grinning, an utterly, delectably wicked grin. "If it was, did it work?"

"One hundred percent," I confessed, a little taken aback.

"By the way." He reached around me to pick up a washcloth, holding it under the faucet before squeezing out the excess moisture. "It wasn't a ploy. I apologize for the snappy tone and general grumpiness. I guess today I was forced to face the fact that my parents are getting old. It was a revelation." As gently as he could, he began cleaning the blood from around my nose and chin while I stood there like a child and pondered what Paul Wilson had been doing in Joyce's apartment.

"Here!" Sylvia returned, with Tylenol and an ice pack. I could have kissed her.

"Thanks." I swallowed the Tylenol and gingerly pressed the ice pack to my face. "Did you get Hazel and Sally's stash?"

"Oh, yes. I gave them to Dennis, and he's making a call."

"How much trouble are they in?" I asked Kade.

"Well, they're not going to get out of this scot free, but who knows? It may be a slap on the wrist or something more severe."

"Can't we keep them out of it? Say we found the drugs?" I knew we couldn't. What the women had been doing was dangerous, and if they weren't going to stop on their own, then we needed to stop them. Despite that, I didn't want to see them arrested.

"Audrey." Kade sighed, and I knew a lecture was imminent.

I headed him off. "Maybe we can go see that

doctor now? See if this really is broken or not?" I took the ice pack off my throbbing nose and examined my reflection in the mirror again. No improvement.

———

My nose was not broken. It was, however, badly bruised, and I'd be sporting two black eyes to go with my swollen nose for a few days, at the very least. We'd just left the urgent care and were heading toward the elevator when Kade said, "Tell me again how this happened. You said a door hit you?"

"So, I was searching Joyce's apartment. I have a theory that she was poisoned, so I figured a quick scout of her place might turn something up."

"And did it?"

"Not poison. Well, not anything that I could easily identify." I shrugged. "But I found something interesting. A letter from this guy called Jay Perry who was threatening legal action against Joyce. He accused her of being responsible for his mother's death."

"Whoa!" Kade stopped walking. "What the..."

"I know!" I nodded a little too vigorously, shards of pain shooting across my face. "I thought I was onto something, too. But Joyce said it was nothing, it had all gone away, and he wasn't suing her."

"Why did he think she was involved in the first place?"

"I take it your mom filled you in on the operation Joyce, Hazel, and Sally had going on? Only it wasn't just Viagra and Valium. It was anything and everything. Obviously, the drugs were the most lucrative for the Vintage Vixens, but they were the ones you turned to if you wanted something you couldn't get your hands on yourself."

"The Vintage Vixens?"

"I made that up," I confessed. "I feel like they need a name, you know? So anyway, Jay's mom, Margaret, is a diabetic, and she wanted chocolate."

"Tell me they didn't give chocolate to a diabetic."

"It was sugar-free."

"And I'm guessing this Jay fella got wind of it?"

"Apparently Joyce told him herself. But she told me it was all sorted, that the lawsuit was dropped—I assume because they discovered Margaret didn't die of a chocolate overdose. Is that even a thing? I mean, as far as ways to go, that wouldn't be bad at all."

"Audrey."

"Right. So, anyway, I was poking around in Joyce's

apartment when all of that came to light. Hazel, Sally, and your mom were there, too. That's when we learned of the drug aspect of their operation. Joyce was the runner, Hazel was inventory, and Sally handled the money. So, I sent them off to retrieve the inventory and take it to you and your dad."

"And where does the door fit into all of this? Because yes, I get that you're clumsy and can trip over thin air, but never before have you walked into a closed door. I find it hard to believe."

"There's a reason you're a detective." I tried to wink, but with half swollen eyes, it wasn't my best effort.

"Audrey."

I got the sense I was testing his patience today, so linking my arm with his, I urged us toward the elevator and continued with my story.

"I was in Joyce's bathroom, wondering if the poison had been topical—that woman has a lot of face creams and potions—when I heard the front door open. There aren't a lot of hiding places in a bathroom, nor a whole lot of time, so I squeezed behind the bathroom door and hoped whoever it was didn't have need to use the facilities."

"Ahhh." I could see he'd worked it out. He knew

where this was going, but I was on a roll and wanted to finish my story.

"Anyway, the guy who'd come in and proceeded to search Joyce's apartment? It was Paul Wilson! He was searching for something specific, and he was cursing up a storm—Kade, he used words that would make a sailor blush—but when he was in the bathroom searching the vanity, he got a call. He seemed really mad and stormed out, and as he left the bathroom, he shoved the door—"

"Which you were hiding behind."

"Which I was hiding behind. And of course I couldn't see him, so I wasn't expecting him to shove the door, so it slammed into my face."

"Oh, babe." He tipped my chin up to examine my bruised and battered face. "He got you a good one."

"The question is," I continued on, "what was he searching for?"

"Why not ask Joyce?"

"Because I haven't seen her since the women left to get the drugs and go to your parents' apartment."

"I think it's time we dropped in for another visit."

"How did you and your dad get on?" I asked. "You were going to do a little investigating of your own, find out about any other deaths on the property?"

"Nothing much has turned up. As expected, when we arrived at the administrative offices and started asking questions, we got stonewalled pretty quickly. Privacy laws and all that—and before you ask, this is out of my jurisdiction. Me being a Firefly Bay Detective does not hold much weight."

"Right."

"Dad is calling in some favors," Kade added. "If anything untoward is happening here, we'll soon know about it."

I chewed my lip, a niggling feeling in the pit of my stomach making me feel sick. "I've had an awful thought," I whispered. "What if Joyce somehow found out that the boss man himself was involved, that he was covering up unexplained deaths, and maybe she approached him about it—she seems to be that type of person, wouldn't think twice about speaking up? And what if he killed her to keep her quiet? And then he was searching her room for any physical evidence she may have had, just to make doubly sure it all goes away."

"It's a theory," Kade agreed. "But we have no evidence, and what's the one thing you learned in PI school?"

"Follow the evidence."

"Follow the evidence," he repeated.

CHAPTER NINE

*K*ade pounded on Hazel's door exactly like a cop. Loud and hard.

"What in the Sam Hill do you want now?" Hazel barked, flinging the door open with a huff.

"Sorry to bother you," I immediately apologized. Her attention shifted from Kade to me, where she did a comical double-take.

"Sweet potato pie!" Hazel exclaimed, unable to hide her shock. "What in tarnation happened to your face?"

I winced as I automatically touched my tender nose. "Oh, just a little mishap with a door," I said with a shrug.

Hazel shook her head in disbelief. "Well, I'll be a

monkey's uncle," she muttered. "I never thought I'd see the day when a door could do that."

I chuckled weakly, feeling a twinge of embarrassment at my swollen nose and black eyes. "It's not too bad, just a little bruising," I said.

Hazel nodded sympathetically, still unable to take her eyes off my bruises. "That's the biggest black eye I've seen since old Zeke got in a fight with a goat back in '54."

"Mind if we come in?" Kade asked.

"Look, honey, I appreciate the visit, but can't you see I'm trying to enjoy my stories?" Hazel gestured toward her TV.

"You know you're in serious trouble, right?" Kade said. "You're facing fourth-degree felony charges for the distribution of Valium."

Sweat beaded on Hazel's forehead, and her face turned ashen. She struggled to take a deep breath, as if the air had suddenly grown thick and heavy.

"Kade," I admonished, stepping forward and taking hold of the older woman's arm, leading her to her recliner. "You're scaring her."

Kade followed, closing the door behind him. "Good," he muttered. "She needs to be scared. What they were doing was foolhardy. Valium alters brain function. Anything could have happened. It's a miracle nothing did."

"We didn't know," Hazel whispered. "We thought we were doing something good."

Kade heaved a frustrated sigh. "Valium is a controlled substance. Using someone else's Valium is illegal, as is selling excess Valium. Possessing large amounts of it indicates an intent to distribute, which results in the harshest legal penalties."

I crouched in front of Hazel. "How much Valium did you have, Hazel? In your stash?"

"Hold on, let me get my book." She struggled to rise from her chair, and Kade wore an alarmed look.

"What?" I hissed. "What's wrong?"

"You documented it?" he asked Hazel.

She nodded. "I'm in charge of inventory."

Kade ran his fingers through his hair. "I can't hear this," he ground out. "You're putting me in a compromised position."

I was confused. What was he talking about? A compromised position?

He spelled it out for me. "If Hazel shows me she kept a ledger with the incoming and outgoing supplies of Valium, then it proves her intent to distribute a Schedule IV controlled substance. Any argument she—*they*—have that they are innocent little old ladies not knowing what they were doing will be blown out of the water."

"Ohhhh." The penny dropped. Kade knew I didn't want to get the women in trouble, and he was doing his best to keep this whole mess on the right side of the law but also not have two old ladies spend the rest of their days in jail. "Best you wait outside. Maybe go check on your dad?" I suggested.

"I think I just might do that." He spun on his heel and stalked out of the apartment, back rigid.

"He seems mad," Hazel observed.

"The slamming of the door gave it away, huh?"

"Just a tad. So, do you want to see this journal or not?"

I shook my head. "No. You need to get rid of it, Hazel. Like, destroy it. One hundred percent destroy it, so it can never be recovered." Kade was right. If Hazel and Sally found themselves in court and I got called as a witness, I'd have to tell the truth. Much better if I didn't see the journal. "Did Joyce have anything that could tie her to the operation you had going on? And Sally?"

"Well, Sally handled the money, so yeah, I'm guessing she kept a running tally on where we were at."

"She needs to get rid of it." I couldn't believe I

was telling these women to destroy evidence. "Who else knew about your operation?"

"The people who gave us their pills and the people who bought them, I suppose." Hazel had recovered from her shock at being labeled a felon and was back on the defensive, her tone waspish. "You're all making this out to be this massive drug dealing den of iniquity, when it was nothing of the sort. A few pills changed hands from time to time, that's all. I don't see what the big deal is."

"The big deal is someone you had business dealings with may have killed Joyce."

"I don't believe it was any of our suppliers or customers. Everyone was more than happy with the arrangement. We had no complaints and no disgruntled customers. Why would you kill the golden goose?"

"That's what we need to find out. Now, what can you tell me about Paul Wilson? What did Joyce have on him?"

Hazel cocked her head. "What do you mean, what did she have on him?"

"After you left Joyce's apartment, Paul turned up, and he was searching for something. Did he know about your pill exchange program? Was he part of it?"

Hazel barked out a laugh. "We're not that stupid. No, he didn't know. And I have no idea why he'd be searching Joyce's apartment. Is he even allowed to do that?"

"I don't think you can be pointing fingers," I pointed out.

"Fair call." Hazel made a move toward her bedroom. "You want this journal or not? Cos if you don't, you'd better vamoose."

"Right!" I gave her a wave goodbye and headed out. Joyce hadn't been at Hazel's apartment, which meant she had to be with Sally. A couple of quick steps and I was knocking on Sally's door. I could hear her television in the background, so she had to be home. I knocked again, louder.

"Oh, hi, Audrey," Sally half yelled over the sound of the television.

"Can I come in?" I shouted back.

Sally ushered me inside, closing the door behind me. "What happened to your face?"

"Run in with a door."

"Hey, Audrey," Joyce called from where she was propped up on cushions in the corner of the sofa, barely taking her eyes off the television. "I hate to be rude, honey, but we have a hot date with *Matlock* in five minutes, so you're gonna have to keep this short." Then her eyes focused on my face, and her jaw dropped. "Holy..." she trailed off, her eyes narrowing into mere slits, and she lifted herself up from the sofa. "Who did this to you? It better not be that man of yours. I may be small, and I may be old, but that doesn't mean I can't whoop his butt."

"You're also dead," I pointed out, waving her to sit back down. "Relax. Kade would never hurt me. No, this was all thanks to a door. Your bathroom door, to be exact."

She frowned, confused. "My bathroom door? What are you even talking about, child?"

"Remember how we were searching your apartment? Well, after you'd gone, Paul Wilson turned up."

"Wee Willy Wilson turned up?" Joyce repeated, clearly puzzled. "What did he want?"

"I didn't exactly ask him. I was hiding behind your bathroom door. But he was looking for something, Joyce. And he was swearing. A lot."

"That sounds about right." She harrumphed, folding her arms over her chest and lowering her chin with a glower.

"What was he searching for?"

"I don't know!" She folded her arms even tighter. She was lying. I didn't know how I knew, I just did.

Shaking my head, I sank down on the sofa next to her and said softly, "Joyce, how can I help you if you won't be straight with me?"

"She holding out on you?" Sally asked, settling into her recliner, remote in hand.

I'd kinda forgotten she was there and turned my attention to her. "Do you have any idea what Paul was looking for in Joyce's apartment?"

"I always thought he had it in for Joyce," Sally said. "Like he had a vendetta against her or something. Not that it bothered Joyce. Water off a duck's back to her. She'd tease him and call him Wee Willy Wilson—to his face—and pretty much disrespect him any chance she got."

While Sally was talking, I watched Joyce, who was nodding at what her friend was saying. "It's true."

"So, you two... what? Just didn't like each other?"

Joyce shrugged, so I turned back to Sally. "Why did Joyce deliberately provoke him? Do you know?"

"You know," Sally gazed out the window. "I'm not really sure. I mean, Joyce could be a bit blunt, a bit cutting if she felt slighted, so maybe he offended her accidentally and from that day forward she just didn't like him?"

"Pure speculation," Joyce snapped. "And as per

usual, Sally has it wrong. Look, if you really want to know, it happened a while back, when Ethel Springs passed away."

"Was her death suspicious?"

"Whose death?" Sally asked.

"Ethel Springs."

"Oh, she was that lovely woman who used to be on Broadway back in the day. She had the most beautiful gowns and jewels." Sally's hands fluttered to her throat. "And she could sing! Boy, she could belt out a tune."

"She was famous?" I asked.

"Yes." Sally nodded, while Joyce shook her head and said, "No."

Joyce rolled her eyes. "Ethel wasn't the leading lady Sally thinks she was, but to give her credit, she was in West Side Story and Hello Dolly."

"On Broadway? In the sixties?" I gasped.

"Yup." Joyce nodded, as if pleased with herself. "She was a supporting player. She said she was the understudy for Anita in the West Side Story— seemed miffed that the role had gone to Chita Rivera."

"Are you serious? That's incredible! But the name Ethel Springs doesn't ring any bells, I'm afraid."

"That's because she went by her stage name. Lila Grace."

"And what does this have to do with Paul Wilson? Were they related or something?"

Joyce snorted. "Or something. Anyway, I used to get Ethel nail polish. She was a real classy lady, and her appearance was very important to her. Her favorite nail polish went missing, so she asked me to get her some more. What I didn't know was that in between her asking for the nail polish and me getting it, she passed away in her sleep. So, when I arrived one afternoon to deliver it, who do you think I found in her room?"

"Who?"

"Paul Wilson!"

"What was he doing?"

"He was wearing one of her gowns, a yellow sequined number with tulle for days. I was used to knocking and walking in, so of course I did just that and there he was, twirling in front of her mirror, admiring himself in her dress."

I blinked, lost for words. "What did you do?"

"I snapped a photo, of course." Joyce sniggered. "It was fortuitous that I even had my camera with me. Old Ray, just down the corridor from Ethel, wanted some photos of his room to send to his family. I was planning on visiting him after I'd delivered Ethel's nail polish."

That's when everything slotted into place. "That's what Paul was looking for. The photo! You were blackmailing him?"

"Do you call it blackmail if money never changed hands?" she said slyly.

"What changed hands? Please don't tell me it was drugs."

"Pft, of course not! No, Wee Willy Wilson was my lackey. I no longer had to run around finding sugar-free chocolate or the right shade of pink nail polish."

"Let me get this straight. Paul Wilson agreed to source all the stuff the residents requested. He'd give it to you, and you'd deliver it to the residents, as if you'd gotten it yourself? And he agreed to that? All because you found him wearing one of Ethel Springs' dresses?"

"He was what?" Sally gasped. Once again, I'd forgotten she was there.

"Where is this photo now?" I asked Joyce.

She shrugged. "Probably still on the roll of film in my camera."

"Roll of... do you mean to say A) your camera is so old it uses film, and B) you never got it developed?"

"I was never into this new age digital nonsense. Now if you don't mind, *Matlock* is starting. Shush."

"But what about Ray's photos? Didn't you say you brought your camera with you that day to take photographs of his room?"

"Lost his nerve after Ethel passed. Said we'd do it another day, but we never did."

"Where's your camera?" I was pretty sure Paul wasn't done searching Joyce's room, and if he stumbled across her camera and realized there was film in it, he just might put two and two together and get four.

"What's that?" Sally asked, cupping a hand to her ear. "You're after Joyce's camera, love? I think I have it here somewhere."

I couldn't hide my surprise. "*You* have it?" To Joyce, I said, "Why does Sally have it?"

"Sure. Let me go grab it for you, pet," Sally said, getting up out of her recliner.

"I gave it to her for safekeeping because I figured something like this might happen," Joyce said. "Paul snooping," she clarified. "Not being murdered."

"Did Paul know about the Valium and Viagra?" I asked for the millionth time.

"Of course not," Joyce scoffed. "I'm not stupid. As

far as he knew, he was getting goods for me. He didn't know I was giving them away."

I narrowed my eyes, squinting. "You must have been turning over a nice little profit."

Joyce dismissed me with a wave of her hand. "What do I need money for? I have everything I need right here." She was lying. The clenching of her hands and the way her eyes wouldn't meet mine told me she was lying.

Leaning forward, I placed a hand on her knee, ignoring the icy shiver from the contact. "Joyce, I need you to be honest with me. If I'm going to find out who killed you, I need to know everything."

"There's nothing to tell." And with that, she disappeared. One second, she was there, the next, gone.

"Here we go, love." Sally returned from the kitchen carrying a box of cereal.

"Oh, sorry, no. I'm not hungry. Thanks, Sally."

"No, silly." Sally giggled. "The camera is in here." She handed me the box, and I peered inside. Sure enough, a black Canon camera sat nestled in the box.

Pulling it out, I held it in my hand and looked at it in wonder. "Wow," I murmured. "I haven't seen one of these since I was a kid." I turned it over in my hands, realizing I had no idea how it worked.

Sally reached out and stopped me from pressing a button on the back. "I wouldn't do that, love. It'll open the back of the camera and expose the film."

"Isn't that what we want to do? Get the film out?"

"No, you have to finish the film first and wind it on, so it's all safe and sound in the little container so that when you open the back, it's not exposed to the light."

"That would be bad?"

She nodded. "If you expose film to the light, it wipes whatever is on the film. Deletes it, if you like."

I turned the camera around in my hands some more, noticed a little number that said eighteen. "Is this how many photos she's taken? Eighteen?"

"That's right."

"How many does she have left?"

"Usually you'd buy a roll of film that could take either twenty-four or thirty-six pictures."

"Which is why she never got the film developed. Because she was only half-way through it."

"I'd assume so." Sally settled back into her recliner.

"And you didn't think it odd that Joyce asked you to hide her camera? Did she tell you why?"

Sally shot me a brief look before turning her attention back to the television, where the opening credits of *Matlock* were rolling. "Who knows? Joyce was always up to something, but on this occasion, I figured she didn't want her son-in-law to get his hands on it."

I jerked in surprise. "Her son-in-law? Why? Does she have compromising photos of him, too?"

"What? No!" Sally waved a hand for me to shush. "A few things had gone missing from her apartment. A vase that was worth a couple of hundred dollars. A yellow push-button phone that, for some reason, she'd kept. One day, she caught him rummaging through her jewelry box. Turns out he'd been stealing from her and pawning the stuff. Claims he needed the money."

"Is that right?"

"See yourself out, love," Sally hinted none too subtly, picking up the remote and turning up the volume.

CHAPTER TEN

"*P*erfect timing, Audrey." Sylvia held the door open for me. I'd raced straight back to the Galloways' apartment with Joyce's camera clutched in my hand, one eye peeled for Paul Wilson. Not that he'd know it was Joyce's camera even if he saw me, but I wasn't sure I could look at him the same way, knowing what I knew.

"Oh?" I stepped inside, casting one last furtive glance over my shoulder before firmly closing the door behind me.

"Yes. Dennis just got a call from his friend. They've got the toxicology report back on Joyce."

My heart raced. This was it. The moment of truth. If Joyce had been poisoned, which was my suspicion, the toxicology report would prove it.

"And?" I pressed.

"I'll let Dennis tell you himself." Sylvia patted my arm. "I don't want to steal his thunder. He's really enjoying himself."

We rounded the corner into the living area. Dennis was seated at the dining table, Kade standing at the windows, looking out at the view.

"They weren't kidding!" Dennis said. "That door got you good."

I'd almost forgotten my face currently resembled a heavy-weight boxer's, but Dennis's reaction brought it back to me tenfold. "I hear you have news?" I sat down opposite him, placing the camera on the table.

"What's that?" he asked.

"You first."

Kade turned at the sound of my voice and joined us, dropping a kiss on the top of my head as he settled onto the chair next to me.

"Joyce Harrison was found to have high levels of tetrahydrozoline in her system," Dennis said, folding his hands together on the tabletop. "Now tetrahydrozoline is a medication found in over-the-counter eye drops and nasal sprays, which sounds harmless enough, but when ingested—taken with food or drink—it can be fatal. Which, in Joyce's case, was true. You were right, Audrey. She was murdered."

Normally, I liked to hear when I was right, but on this occasion, not so much. "Eye drops you say?"

Dennis nodded. "And nasal sprays. Both easy to source."

I was wracking my brain, trying to remember if I'd seen either of those items in Joyce's apartment, but to be honest, I hadn't known what I was looking for, so it was entirely possible I'd skimmed right over them.

"Your turn." Dennis tapped the table. "What's with the camera?"

"It turns out Joyce has a compromising photo of Paul Wilson. She was running an errand for a resident, Ethel Springs. Only when she turned up to Ethel's room to deliver the goods, she'd passed away. But Paul Wilson was there. Wearing one of Ethel's gowns."

"A nightgown?" Sylvia asked, puzzled.

"No, like an evening gown. Or a ball gown, I guess. Ethel used to be on Broadway. Her stage name was Lila Grace, and I'm guessing she kept some of her costumes."

"So, you're saying"—Dennis leaned back in his

chair—"that Paul Wilson is what? A cross dresser? A drag queen? Gay? Trans?"

"Not that there's anything wrong with any of those," Sylvia hastened to add.

I shrugged. "I'm not saying anything. I have no idea why he was wearing Ethel's dress. But what I do know is that in some wicked twist of fate, Joyce had her camera with her that day, and when she burst in on him, she snapped a photo. The film hasn't been developed yet."

"That's what Paul was searching Joyce's apartment for," Kade said, reaching the same conclusion I had. "A photograph."

"Only he doesn't know that the photograph doesn't exist. Not yet anyway. Only the negative. And is it even a negative if the film hasn't been developed? And where would we get this developed? Everything is digital nowadays."

"Did Joyce tell you all of this?" Kade asked, picking up the camera and turning it over in his hands.

"Uh-huh. Apparently, she was blackmailing Paul."

"That crafty old w—"

"Now Dennis, language," Sylvia scolded before he could get the word out.

"Witch," he grumbled. "I was going to say witch."

I chuckled. "Yeah, well, the blackmail stakes weren't high. No money changed hands. Instead, she got Paul to source all the items residents had requested. So, it wasn't Joyce who was running around buying sugar-free chocolate or nail polish or whatever was on the wish list. It was Paul."

"And these residents—were they paying her?" Kade asked.

"She says not, but I'm not sure I believe her," I admitted. "She got all defensive and disappeared when I asked her about it. Sally told me that Joyce's son-in-law had been stealing from her and that's why Joyce had given the camera to Sally for safekeeping, to make sure it didn't go missing."

"Sylvia, love, get me a marker from the kitchen drawer," Dennis said, picking up the camera and turning it over in his hands.

"What do you need a marker for?" she asked.

"To keep track of our suspects. So far, we have this Jay Perry chap, who was threatening a lawsuit, and clearly Paul Wilson had motive, plus I'd be interested to know more about this son-in-law."

Dennis was spot on. Those were my top three suspects, too. Even though Joyce had said Jay had dropped his complaint, we should still talk to him.

As for Paul Wilson, we needed to get this film developed. Maybe Joyce didn't have the blackmail material she thought she had. Either way, Paul didn't know that. Did she push him too far? Demanding more and more until the only way out was to get rid of her?

I shook my head. "I don't know," I whispered to myself. "It seems too farfetched."

Kade leaned in close, his breath hot on my cheek. "The whole Wilson blackmail thing?" His voice was as low as mine.

"Yeah," I whispered back. "I mean, so what if he was wearing a dress? That's hardly scandalous, not nowadays."

"I think the problem for Wilson is that he was trying on a resident's clothing. On premises. While on duty. Something like that could cost him his job."

"Of course!" It wasn't that Paul was worried about the photo getting out. He was worried someone would recognize where the photo was taken... in Ethel Springs' room.

My phone began vibrating in my pocket. Seb was calling. Again. Which could only mean one thing. Amanda. Plastering a smile on my face, I accepted the video call.

"Hi, Seb." I tried to smile despite my face hurting. "I'm here with Kade and his parents."

"What on earth happened to your face?" Seb demanded.

"Mom, Mom, Mom!" Bandit scrambled over Seb's shoulder, peering at the screen.

"Hi, Bandit. Don't worry, I'm okay. I got hit in the face with a door."

"Hit in the... with a door..." Seb needed a moment to gather his thoughts.

"I'm staaaarving," Thor wailed in the background. "Feeeeeed meeeeeee."

"Oh, dear." I couldn't help but giggle. Thor was putting on an Oscar worthy performance.

"He's fine," Seb assured me over the racket Thor was making. "Hang on, let me flip you around." He switched the camera so I could see Thor, who was stretched out on his back on the floor. When he saw the phone aimed his way, he stopped his wailing. "Are you filming me?" He immediately began grooming himself, licking his paw and rubbing it over his face. "Hang on."

"See?" Seb was back. "All good. He's just being a drama queen, and I should know. I'm one, too."

"What's up?"

"A box arrived." The way he said it, his voice devoid of emotion, told me this wasn't a good thing.

"A box? Who from?"

"Guess."

"Amanda." It wasn't difficult. I wasn't expecting any deliveries, and Amanda was already muscling her way into my wedding planning during my absence. I pinched the bridge of my nose, then immediately regretted it as twin barbs of red hot lightning shot down the bridge. I hissed, releasing my fingers. "Go ahead. Open it."

Seb propped the phone on the counter, lining it up with the dining room table where a large white box sat. Opening the box, Seb began lifting out multiple smaller boxes. I leaned closer. "What is that?"

"These," Seb said, holding one of the smaller boxes in the palm of his hand and opening it, "are cake samples."

I blinked. I'd never heard of cake samples before.

"I'm not sure I understand. Amanda sent me cake?"

Seb nodded, continuing to lift the smaller boxes out of the larger one. There had to be at least fifty. "These are wedding cake samples," Seb explained.

"So you can choose what type of cake and flavor you want."

"Oh." I nodded, nonplussed. "I haven't given it much thought."

Seb shot me a look. "Which, I think, is Amanda's point. She has arranged for"—he read off the label —"Blissful Bites Bakery to send you a collection to choose from. You know, do you want mud cake or sponge or fruit cake? And then, do you prefer chocolate or vanilla or strawberry?"

I rolled my eyes as Seb just filled me in on Amanda's latest antics with my wedding planning. It's like she's trying to take over the whole thing! I mean, I appreciate her enthusiasm, but come on, can't a bride get a little bit of say in her own wedding? I swear, if she suggests one more thing, I might just elope and call it a day. And to think, I even hired Seb to help me out, and she's still managing to bulldoze her way into everything.

"What is it?" Sylvia whispered.

"Babe?" Kade asked from next to me. He'd been watching. He could see for himself what Amanda had sent.

"I didn't ask her to do that," I said. "We're not even there to taste the cakes. Why did she send them?"

Seb shrugged. "I think she's trying to be helpful?"

My temper flared. "Well, it's not helpful. She's not helpful. This isn't helping!" I stood up, my chair almost toppling over.

"Audrey? Where'd you go? Why am I looking at the ceiling?" Seb asked.

I stalked away, leaving my phone on the table, the call still open. My mind was a jumble of thoughts, none of them pleasant. I'd allowed myself to be distracted by Joyce's murder, burying myself in the investigation rather than face up to what was happening back home. But one thing was obvious. I needed to deal with Amanda, or she was going to ruin my entire wedding. Or at the very least, suck every last ounce of joy out of it.

"Hey, Seb, it's Kade." Kade picked up the call while I bolted for the front door, not sure where I was going, only that I needed fresh air.

"Audrey!" Sylvia hurried after me.

"I just need a minute." My fingers were all thumbs as I struggled to get the door open.

"Here, let me." Sylvia eased me to one side and opened the door. "Come on, let's take a walk. You can fill me in on this sister-in-law of yours."

I shot ahead, eventually slowing when I realized

I didn't know where I was going. With the weight of the world on my shoulders, I turned to Sylvia, waiting for her to catch up.

"Sorry." This wasn't how I wanted my first meeting with Kade's parents to go. First the ghost stuff, now Amanda. Why couldn't I be normal? Why couldn't this be perfect?

"Hey." Sylvia linked her elbow with mine and guided me toward a side entrance off the main foyer. "Never apologize for being upset. We're all human. We all have emotions. It's what you do with them that matters."

I could see why Sylvia Galloway had made an excellent schoolteacher. She had a way of calming you. And what she said made perfect sense. I decided if I wanted to have an open and honest relationship with my future mother-in-law, then my guards had to come down. It was time to go all in.

"I really wanted this weekend to be different, you know?" I blurted. "I mean, I'm sure Kade's already told you what a klutz I am. I didn't want to give you even more of a bad impression, but I feel like everything is spinning out of control."

"Being *clumsy*"—she stressed the word—"is not a character flaw. No matter what your sister-in-law says. I've been looking forward to meeting you for so long, and Audrey? I'm not disappointed. Dennis and I love you. But we knew we would because our son does. The first time Kade mentioned you to us, when we were still in Australia, I knew. I knew he'd found the one. I could hear it in his voice. How much he loved you, how happy he was, and honey? That's all a momma bear wants for her son. All of this Amanda nonsense is just that—nonsense. She's just noise. Don't give her that space in your head. But can I give you just the teeniest bit of advice?"

"Please do. I'm at my wit's end with her."

"You need to deal with it. You need to have a frank discussion with her. Set boundaries. And let your family know what these boundaries are so they can support you—and her—moving forward. They're probably not even aware you feel this way. Am I right? Because you don't want to upset them."

She was right. Of course, she was right.

"You're right." I put my hand over Sylvia's where it was looped through my elbow. "Let's go back. I need to make a call."

We'd just returned to the apartment when we ran into Kade and Dennis, leaving.

"Oh, where are you off to?" I asked. "I came back for my phone."

Kade pulled it from the back pocket of his jeans

and handed it to me. "Seb says not to worry your pretty little head about the cakes. He's going to talk to us both when we get back about what sort of cake we think we'd like, and then he'll narrow it down from there and get us samples. You don't have to taste over fifty cakes."

I gave a tight smile. "Thanks."

"We're off to see Jay Perry." Dennis elbowed his way past his son, forcing me to back up to let him out or risk getting trampled.

"You know where he lives?"

"He's here. Playing golf. He kept up his mother's membership."

"How do you even know that?" I followed behind. No way I was going to miss this.

"Dad's been busy on the phone," Kade told me. "In a little under an hour, he had Jay Perry's number, called him, and learned he was here playing golf."

"Today of all days," Dennis interjected.

"It could be a coincidence," I said.

"If it's a coincidence, I'll be a monkey's uncle."

I never thought I'd be playing golf, but here I was, standing on the green with a golf club in my hand.

How Dennis had talked me into it, I didn't know, but through some form of sorcery or magic, he'd convinced me that a round of golf was an excellent idea. Since Jay was only on the third tee, we had plenty of time to catch up with him.

"Okay, Audrey, just aim for the ball and swing," Kade instructed, standing next to me with his arms crossed.

I took a deep breath and swung the club. But instead of hitting the ball, the club flew out of my hands and landed in the nearby bushes.

"Whoops," I said, trying to hide my embarrassment.

Dennis let out a hearty laugh. "Looks like we have a natural talent on our hands, Kade."

Kade just shook his head, trying to hide his smile. "Don't worry, Audrey. Everyone has to start somewhere."

I walked over to the bushes to retrieve my club, trying my best not to trip over my own feet in the process. This was going to be a long game.

After retrieving the club, I returned to the tee and eyeballed the dimpled white ball. How hard could this be? Dennis and Kade had hit their respective balls with ease and were waiting patiently for me to have my turn. Sylvia, upon learning that we were actually going to play golf and not just talk to Jay, had balked and headed back to the apartment, declaring golf was not her sport and admonishing her husband not to overdo it. I wished I'd followed her lead and opted out.

"All right, Audrey, just swing at the ball and let it fly!" Kade said, grinning from ear to ear.

I raised my club, trying to look confident, but I couldn't shake the feeling that this wasn't going to end well. Naturally, I wasn't wrong. I swung and missed the ball, spinning myself around in a circle so hard I almost fell over.

"I think this is going to be a very entertaining game." Dennis chuckled.

My face burned as I regained my balance and stalked up to the ball. I had never felt so clumsy in my entire life.

Things only got worse from there. Every time I swung, the ball went in the opposite direction, hitting trees and even once landing in a sand trap. Kade and Dennis tried to give me pointers, but it was clear I was a lost cause.

As I groaned in frustration at my latest swing, Kade and Dennis exchanged a knowing look. They were trying to be supportive, but I could tell they were also struggling to keep a straight face.

"Okay, Audrey, let's try this," Kade said, placing his hands on my shoulders. "Just take a deep breath and relax. You've got this."

I nodded, trying to focus on his words of encouragement. Maybe if I could just calm down, I could actually hit the ball for once. With newfound determination, I raised my club and swung. And to my absolute surprise, the ball went flying through the air, straight toward the hole.

I couldn't believe it. I hit it! I turned to Kade and Dennis, who were both cheering me on with big grins on their faces.

"That's my girl!" Kade shouted, giving me a high-five.

I laughed with relief. Maybe I wasn't a total disaster at golf after all. The rest of the game went by in a blur of swings and misses, but I didn't care. I had always thought golf looked like an easy sport. I mean, how hard could it be to hit a small white ball into a hole in the ground? Turned out, it was way harder than it looked.

As we walked off the green at the end of the game, Dennis put his arm around me and gave a playful nudge.

"You know, Audrey, for a first-timer, you're not half bad," he said, winking at me.

I grinned, feeling proud of myself for overcoming my initial embarrassment and having a good time despite the fact that I was covered in dirt and sweat, my hair sticking up in all directions.

"We didn't catch up with Jay, though," I pointed out. It had taken us a lot longer to get through nine holes of golf than Dennis and Kade had expected.

"He's waiting for us here." Dennis jerked his head toward the Sunset Café.

"What? How?"

"When he invited us to join him on the green, we thought we could easily catch up," Dennis said. "When it became apparent that wasn't going to happen, I sent him a message, and he said he'd wait for us here."

"He invited us to play golf with him?" I ground out. I thought the golf had been Dennis's harebrained scheme, and I'd gone along with it to humor him.

"He invited me and dad," Kade said. The penny dropped. His unspoken words echoed loud and clear in my head. I had not been invited. I'd messed up their plans. This was meant to have been a father-son bonding moment, and I'd barged in like a wrecking ball and ruined it.

"Umm." I touched my palms to my cheeks,

feeling the heat of the day emanating from my skin. "I think I might get cleaned up. I feel gross." In more ways than one.

"You do look like you've caught a bit of sun, love." Dennis was all concern. "Go on ahead. Kade and I can talk to Jay."

I didn't think it was possible to feel any worse than I already did, but what do you know, I could. I was swanning around like this was my investigation, bossing everyone around, insisting on being in on the action. Dennis Galloway was a retired police officer and his super hot son, who was watching me with an enigmatic expression on his face, was a detective. They weren't idiots. They didn't need me.

I hurried back to the Galloways' apartment, feeling embarrassed and foolish. How could I have been so clueless? Of course, Kade had wanted to spend some quality time with his dad, and I had gone and ruined it by insisting on tagging along.

CHAPTER ELEVEN

I hadn't meant to fall asleep. I'd returned to the apartment, caught sight of my sunburned and bruised face, and wanted to cry, and I wasn't a crier. Instead, I'd taken a shower, which helped somewhat, then I'd stretched out on the bed, telling myself I'd have a five-minute rest before joining Sylvia, who was puttering about in the kitchen. She'd taken one look at me and said she'd move dinner reservations to tomorrow night instead.

The weight of the bed dipping near my hip had me opening my eyes to discover the room was dark. Where had the sun gone?

"Garp?" I garbled into the darkness.

"I'm not sure if you're asking what time is it? Or where are you?" Kade chuckled, his hand coming to rest on my hip. "Mom said you were resting. Are you okay?"

"I'm sorry about today. I'm such an idiot. I barged my way into plans you had with your dad."

"What are you even talking about?" He sounded genuinely puzzled.

"Today. Golf." I was choked up with emotion. The nap hadn't helped, and right now I yearned for home, to be in familiar surroundings, have Ben tell me to pull my head out of my butt, have Bandit lavish me with unconditional love, and Thor demanding to be fed. I missed home.

"You didn't ruin anything, if that's what you're thinking." Kade lay down beside me, entwining his fingers with mine. "Having you join us for golf wasn't a problem if that's what's gotten into your gorgeous head. Are you forgetting Dad invited you? Actually, having you join us forced Dad to take it easy. You took so long at each shot that he sat down and rested at every hole."

"Oh. That's good then."

"Audrey." He heaved a sigh. "What's going on? You've been out of sorts all day."

"Nothing. Everything's fine," I lied.

"Everything is not fine." He cursed, rolling toward me. I could just see his outline in the dim room. "Audrey..." He paused, the silence ominous. "Are you getting cold feet?"

I frowned. "No, my feet aren't cold." What an odd question. Then I realized what he meant and felt all sorts of a fool all over again. "Oh! You mean about the wedding!"

"Don't you want to marry me anymore?" His voice was deep, low, and full of anguish.

I blindly reached out, groping for his face in the dark, until I eventually managed to cup his cheeks in my hands. "I want to marry you more than anything," I whispered, voice thick with tears. "I love you."

"Thank God," he said. "I love you too." The kiss that followed was full of love and promise and heat and passion. He was my everything. And I realized I'd been hurting him. With my frustration with Amanda and the wedding planning, I *had* been feeling very anti-wedding. But not anti-marriage.

"It's just..." I eventually whispered against his lips.

"It's just what?"

"The wedding. I want to get *married*. It's just the wedding itself. It's a lot."

He heaved a sigh, wrapped his arms around me, and rolled, pulling me to lie on top of him. "When we get home"—he snuggled my head into the crook of his neck and shoulder—"we're having a family meeting. A sit down with everyone. Some ground rules are going to be established."

"You talked to your mom," I said against his neck. His chest rumbled underneath me as he chuckled.

"My mom told me I needed to step up and support you more."

"But this isn't your fault," I protested, lifting my head.

"It's not yours either," he pointed out. "I know you're frustrated because Amanda isn't listening. She's not hearing you. We'll make her hear together."

"Will you use your scary cop voice?"

"I will definitely use my scary cop voice," he promised, squeezing me tight.

"Dinner!" Sylvia bellowed.

"Oh my gosh, what time is it?" I scrambled out of Kade's embrace and off the bed, knocking the bedside lamp onto the floor. "Are you kidding me!"

A click, then a soft golden glow illuminated the room. Kade propped on one elbow, watching me as I staggered about.

"Is everything else okay?" he asked.

"What do you mean?" I eventually found my shoes and sat on the bed to pull them on.

"Nothing else is bothering you? Other than the wedding, which isn't really the wedding, more Amanda. Did I get that right, or is it wishful thinking?"

I looked at him, aghast that I'd led him to believe I didn't want to marry him. "Babe, marrying you is the one thing I *am* sure of. Look." I turned my attention back to getting the right shoe on the right foot. "Coming to Chicago to meet your parents was a big deal. I was really nervous."

"I know."

"And then within minutes of meeting them, I outed myself talking to a ghost. You have no idea how stressful that was."

"I have a fair idea."

"And now we're all investigating Joyce's death together? This has been the most bizarre trip I've ever been on."

"And you miss Bandit and Thor."

I nodded, feeling a little misty eyed. Who'd have thought I'd miss those two balls of fluff this much? Kade crawled across the bed and hugged me, burying his face against my neck.

"And then I nearly broke my nose with a door, and to top it all off, I got sunburned today."

"No wonder you needed a nap."

I could barely make out what he said, his voice muffled against my skin.

"Come on, get moving. I don't want to keep your mom waiting. Not after she made dinner for us."

Heaving an exaggerated sigh, he disengaged and climbed off the bed, holding out a hand to haul me to my feet. Hand in hand, we made our way to the dining room, remnants of a glorious sunset barely visible through the living room windows.

"You missed a corker of a sunset," Dennis said, already seated at the table.

"Sorry. I fell asleep."

Dennis squinted at me. "How's the nose? Looks like the swelling's gone down a bit. But you caught the sun today."

"I know." *But thanks for pointing it out.*

"Dennis," Sylvia scolded. "Mind your manners."

"What?" he protested. "She did."

"And doesn't need you pointing it out, for goodness' sake. Audrey, honey, I have a wonderful cream that'll take the sting right out and soothe the redness. Remind me to grab it for you after dinner."

"Thanks, that'd be great."

She placed a plate piled high with chicken fried steak, mashed potato, and gravy in front of me. My stomach rumbled on cue. "This looks delicious."

"Mom makes the best chicken steak," Kade said, patting my knee under the table.

After everyone was served and Sylvia was seated, we dug in. Kade wasn't wrong. I could see where he got his culinary skills from.

"So." I waved my fork at no-one in particular, and a blob of mashed potato landed on the table. I ignored the fact that I was now flinging food around my in-laws' dining room, casually scooped it up, and put it back on my plate. "Did you guys meet up with Jay after all that?"

"Yup." Dennis mimicked my gesture, pointing his fork at me. Only he did it without making a mess. "Nice chap. Not responsible for Joyce's death."

"How do you know that?"

"He wasn't here," Kade said. "He arrived to play golf after Joyce had died."

"Just because he didn't start his game of golf until after she died doesn't mean he wasn't here at Torres Place," I felt compelled to point out.

"The receipt he had for gas puts him at a gas station across town," Dennis said. "Unless he's found a way to teleport, he didn't have enough time to drive over here, administer eye drops to Joyce's food, drive back across town to get gas, and then come back—again—just to establish an alibi."

"Oh, there you are. I've been looking for you." Joyce appeared, making me jump. I lost my grip on my knife, and it clattered to the floor.

"Audrey?" Sylvia asked. "Everything okay?"

"I'm fine," I grunted as I bent to retrieve the knife. Pushing back my chair, I went to rinse it at the sink. "Joyce just turned up." Of course, Dennis and Sylvia, upon learning that Joyce's ghost had graced us with her presence, both gushed out an over effusive greeting.

"How's the face?" Joyce leaned in close, examining my bruises and sunburn.

"It's fine."

"It doesn't look fine. If anything, you look worse than before."

"Thanks," I snapped. "Maybe if you'd told me you were blackmailing Paul Wilson, none of this would have happened. I wouldn't have been in your apartment when Paul turned up, searching for, oh I don't know, maybe a photograph you were using to blackmail him. I wouldn't have been hiding behind the bathroom door, and it wouldn't have hit me in the face. What do you have to say about that, hmm?"

"That you should have found a better hiding place." She shrugged. "What's this photograph you're talking about? I don't have a photograph." She was lying. Again! She'd told me herself that she'd taken a photo of Paul wearing one of Ethel's ballgowns.

I picked up the camera Sylvia had moved from the kitchen table to the counter and waved it at Joyce. "Does this ring any bells?"

"Oh, there it is. I was wondering what I'd done with that." Joyce went to take the camera from me, but her hand passed right through it.

"You left it with Sally for safekeeping. You were worried your son-in-law might steal it."

Joyce jerked, as if I'd slapped her, swiveling away and crossing to the living room windows, placing her face through the glass as she peered outside.

"Sally must be confused," Joyce said. "She asked to borrow the camera, and honestly, I forgot she had it."

"Why are you lying?" I said softly, crossing to stand by her side. "Look, I know you took a photo of Paul wearing Ethel's dress that you used to blackmail him into doing your bidding."

"I was thinking on my feet that day." She puffed out her chest, clearly pleased with herself. "I told him the photo would never see the light of day if he did my bidding."

"Which was?"

"That he sourced the items our clients needed."

"Like Viagra and Valium?"

Joyce shook her head. "Are you insane? I didn't want him involved in that. No, the other stuff. Chocolate. Nail polish. Nora Roberts' latest bestseller. That sort of thing."

"So, Paul didn't know about the drugs?"

"Of course not. Why would he? It's not like we did it often."

I frowned. "What do you mean?"

"The Viagra. Not a lot of demand. And certainly not many people wanting to sell their pills, if you know what I mean."

"And the Valium?"

She shrugged. "Same deal. It's not like we did a roaring trade. We'd pick up a few pills here and there and sell them on, but it's not the big drug ring you seem to be inferring."

I turned to the dining table where Sylvia, Dennis, and Kade were all watching me talk to thin air.

"What's she saying?" Dennis asked.

"That not many pills changed hands. That it's

not the big drug operation we're inferring. Dennis, how many pills were in the stash Sylvia gave you?"

"One four-pill blister pack of Viagra, two pills missing. One box of 5 mg diazepam, fifty tablets in total, but only one half empty blister pack left."

I glared at Kade. He'd led me to believe the women had a stockpile of illicit drugs. Two Viagra pills and maybe five Valium pills were hardly a haul, and certainly not enough to have them arrested for drug dealing.

"It's still a felony to sell prescription medications that are not yours," Kade responded to my glare.

"Yes, but this is hardly going to see them spend jail time! You made me think they were headed to the big house."

"I needed them to be scared. What they were doing was outright stupid."

"He's right," Dennis chimed in. "Not only illegal, but dangerous."

"Yes, I know," I cried. "I'm not the one who needs a lecture."

Kade and Dennis both had the grace to look sheepish while Sylvia appeared to share my ire.

"Did you boys intentionally mislead Audrey?"

Dennis sat back, raising his hands in surrender. "Hey, it wasn't me! I didn't tell Audrey anything. If someone at this table led her to believe the pills trading hands were more numerous than they actually were, well, it wasn't me." He one hundred percent threw his son under the bus.

"Kade!" Sylvia scolded. "That was not nice. Audrey has a lot on her plate right now. She's in an unfamiliar environment, with people she's only just met, and you're playing silly games to frighten some old women into walking the straight and narrow? Now is not the time."

"Mom," Kade started, but Sylvia cut him off.

"Don't you Mom me. You apologize to your fiancée."

"Sorry, Audrey."

I couldn't help it. I giggled. The giggle escalated into laughter that I couldn't control. Tears rolled down my cheeks, and I wrapped my arms around my middle because my ribs ached from laughing so hard. Kade looked like a little schoolboy being chastised, not by his teacher, but by his mom. Of course, my laughter was infectious, and soon the entire table joined in my mirth.

The laughter broke the tension, and Kade waved me back to the table. "Come and finish your dinner."

I sat back down, Joyce hovering at the end of the table. "Do you think Paul killed me?" she asked.

I shrugged. "It certainly seems he had motive."

"What's she saying?" Dennis stage whispered.

"She's wondering if Paul Wilson killed her."

Dennis leaned back in his chair and stroked his clean-shaven chin, as if caressing an invisible beard. "Considering she was blackmailing him, that definitely gives him motive. As for opportunity, we're going to have to trace his movements."

"He let himself into Joyce's apartment with a key, yet he wasn't lugging around a massive key ring, so I'm thinking he has a master key."

"Meaning he can let himself in and out of anyone's apartment," Dennis finished for me.

"You know what we should do next?" Sylvia said. "We should get that film developed. If that is what he was looking for in Joyce's apartment, maybe there's more on it than a photo of him in a dress."

"That alone is pretty damning," Kade pointed out. "Like I said earlier, something like that could cost him his job."

"Yes, but he also knew all he had to do was destroy the photo and the problem would go away. He didn't need to kill Joyce," Sylvia shot back.

Kade wasn't convinced. "She could still tell people."

"But would they believe her? Joyce seems to have

a bit of a reputation as a prankster. Paul could spin it, make it sound like a fanciful story made up by a woman wanting to pull your leg," Dennis said.

"Audrey." Sylvia grabbed my arm, her face lit up with excitement. "Tomorrow, you and I are going to go get that film developed. The boys can do some snooping as to Paul's whereabouts at the time of Joyce's death." She let go of my arm and looked at her husband. "Do we know when the poison was administered? Was it fast acting?"

He nodded. "Toxicology shows she still had tetrahydrozoline in her system, meaning it was ingested prior to her death."

"How prior? Breakfast this morning? Or dinner last night?"

"Breakfast this morning."

Sylvia nodded. "Right. You two need to go to the Sunset Café in the morning and find out if Paul Wilson was there. Do they have CCTV? The cameras may have caught him in the act."

I was a little taken aback that I hadn't thought of that. I mean, Private Investigating 101, check CCTV footage.

CHAPTER TWELVE

*B*right morning sunlight peeking through the curtains pulled me awake. Reluctantly, and with a heartfelt groan, I rolled onto my back. It was odd to sleep without Bandit and Thor plastered all over me. Yet, despite my aching face, I'd had a good night's rest. Then I heard it—an empty silence that told me Kade was gone. Cracking open one eye, I looked at the empty pillow next to me. Yep. Kade was gone all right, but there was a note written in his familiar scrawl. He'd left me breakfast in the kitchen.

Shooting out of bed, I rushed to the kitchen, desperately praying I hadn't slept in too late and breakfast was cold. Relief flooded me when I found a plate overflowing with still-warm pancakes and fresh fruit waiting. Sitting at the table, I savored each bite and thought of the amazing man who'd put this meal together before leaving. His love surrounded me like a warm embrace, preparing me for the day ahead. Sylvia and I had plans to head out and get the film developed from Joyce's camera, and I was genuinely looking forward to spending time with my mother-in-law to be.

"Oh, you're up!" Sylvia bustled through with a load of laundry in her arms. "How did you sleep?"

"Like a log," I confessed. "Kade left a note that he and Dennis have already headed out?"

"You know"—Sylvia glanced at the clock on the wall—"you only just missed them. They've been gone all of five minutes."

"Yeah, I figured as much. The pancakes are still warm."

Continuing her journey to the tiny mudroom slash laundry, Sylvia said, "You're looking much better today."

"I'm feeling better too," I confessed. The swelling had receded, and the two black eyes had started to fade, leaving the purple bruises dusting each eyelid to appear almost like eyeshadow. I quite liked it. Not that I'd go around slamming my face into doors to achieve the effect regularly. And the cream Sylvia had given me before going to bed last night had worked like magic, taking most of the redness out of my sunburned cheeks. I felt almost human again.

After I'd finished my breakfast, Sylvia and I headed out to the store to get Joyce's film developed. We handed the camera over to the clerk, who told us it would take about an hour. Sylvia and I looked at each other and then around the store, unsure of what to do to kill the time.

"Hey, why don't we go look at wedding dresses?" Sylvia suggested with a smile.

I looked at her with surprise and a certain degree of trepidation. "Wedding dresses?"

"Yes, why not? You're getting married soon, and we have an hour to kill. Come on, it'll be fun!" She was already pulling me toward the door. "There's a boutique a couple of doors down."

I laughed at Sylvia's enthusiasm. She was right. Finding the perfect dress had been a stress point for me. Amanda had been pestering me non-stop to set up an appointment to try on dresses in Firefly Bay. Of course, she expected to be invited, along with my mom and Laura. Maybe looking at dresses with Sylvia would help ease some of that stress. A trial run wasn't such a bad idea.

As we walked into the boutique, I couldn't help

but feel a little intimidated by the rows upon rows of white and ivory gowns. I had never been much of a girly-girl, and the thought of trying on dresses and discussing fabrics and cuts was a little daunting.

"This one looks beautiful." Sylvia held up a dress with a long train and intricate lace details.

I took the dress from her and held it up against my body. "It's beautiful, but I'm not sure it's 'me.'"

We continued browsing, nothing really leaping out at me. Sylvia was like a kid in a candy store, pulling out dresses left and right while I tried to keep up with her. Then I saw it—the most beautiful dress I had ever laid eyes on. It was simple yet elegant, with a flowing train and delicate beading. Without thinking, I rushed toward it, my feet tangling in a nearby display and sending me crashing to the floor. The whole boutique went silent as everyone turned to look at the clumsy bride-to-be lying on the ground.

But, true to form, Sylvia was there to save the day, helping me up and dusting me off as I tried to regain my dignity. One of the boutique attendants, who'd witnessed my spectacular sprawl, hurried over. She was mid-forties, caramel colored hair that hung dead straight, reaching just above her shoulders. She wore a pair of tortoiseshell glasses perched on the tip of her nose.

"Hey there! Let me tell you about this gorgeous bridal gown I'm absolutely in love with. It's an A-line design that's soft, flowing, and just perfect for that magical wedding day. The dress features sparkling floral lace and laser-cut botanical lace that sits perfectly over a plunging V-shaped neckline. The way the two types of lace combine is just breathtaking!

But that's not all. The shimmering tulle skirt of this dress really sets it apart. It has a hidden high slit on the right side that is so subtle, yet so stunning. Trust me, your guests won't be able to take their eyes off it. It's truly mesmerizing."

"It's gorgeous." I sighed, reaching out to touch it but quickly dropping my arm before my fingers made contact with the fabric.

"Would you like to try it on?"

I eyed the dress. Half of me was terrified to try it on. What if it didn't fit? What if I got stuck, half in, half out, and tore it? What if it looked absolutely awful on me? But this dress had called to me from the sea of white tulle and lace. It would be a crime *not* to try it on.

"You know." I paused and looked at the woman. "What's your name?"

She smiled. She knew she had me. "Helen."

"Hi, Helen. I'm Audrey, and this is my mother-in-law, Sylvia. And yes, I'd love to try on the dress."

"You're going to look amazing," Helen gushed, scooping the gown into her arms and leading the way to the dressing room at the back of the store. There was a small, square podium in the middle of the room, with two cubicles off to one side. A two-seater love seat upholstered in plush pink velvet sat against the wall.

"Okay, Audrey, let's get you set up in here." Helen directed me into one of the cubicles. "Sylvia, why don't you have a seat? We won't be long."

Inside the cubicle, I began undressing, eyeing the gown Helen had hung on the hook on the wall. It was bigger than I'd realized.

Helen chuckled. "Don't worry, that's why I'm here. To help you into the dress."

Standing self-consciously in my underwear, I followed Helen's instructions to raise my arms, then she expertly shimmied the dress over the top of my head.

"Oh my gosh," I whispered, staring at myself in the mirror. The dress was stunning. It had been gorgeous on the hanger, but now, wearing it? I was speechless. Helen began doing it up, tugging and pulling and fussing until it was as perfect as she could get it.

"You look beautiful," she said softly, her eyes meeting mine in the mirror. "Ready to go show your mother-in-law?"

I nodded, and Helen pulled back the curtain with a flourish, directing me to the podium. I made my way toward it, concentrating hard on not tripping. The dress was heavy and long, but once I was on the podium and facing the enormous mirror, I got the full effect of the dress, and it stole my breath away.

Sylvia's eyes lit up as she looked at me. "Oh, Audrey, you look stunning! Kade is going to love it."

Relief and excitement warred within me. I'd found it. The perfect dress. I twirled around, admiring myself in the mirror. "Do you really think so?" I asked, my voice tinged with uncertainty. I loved it, I really did, but it was the first dress I'd tried on. Wasn't I meant to try on dozens?

"Absolutely," Sylvia replied without hesitation. "You look like a princess."

I blushed, a smile spreading across my face. "I do, don't I?"

Sylvia stepped forward and wrapped me in a warm hug. "You know, Audrey, I'm so happy that you're going to be a part of our family. You and Kade are perfect for each other. It warms my heart."

Tears pricked at the corners of my eyes. "Me too." I sniffed. "Now let's get me out of this dress before the unthinkable happens and I rip it or something."

I left the boutique with a spring in my step. The dress was paid for, and I'd arranged for it to be shipped to Firefly Bay. I'd snapped a picture and sent it to Seb.

I found it! The perfect dress.

You look amazeballs!

So happy.

Where? How? I didn't think you were going to go dress shopping in Chicago?

Funny story. Had some time to kill and popped into this boutique place with my future mother-in-law, and there it was. The one.

Yes, way to go, girl!

Needs some minor alterations.
Know anyone?

Do I know anyone? Do you know
who you're talking to? Of course I
do. Leave it with me. Bringing it
home with you or shipping?

Shipping. They have to order it in.

Coolio. I'll let my seamstress know
we'll be in need of his services.

Thanks, Seb. Talk later. Gotta run.

Byeeee

I was on cloud nine, practically skipping down the sidewalk, when a thought occurred to me. Stopping in my tracks, I turned to Sylvia. "I hope Mom isn't going to be upset she wasn't here." I chewed my lip, worried Mom's feelings would be hurt. She and Laura had both expressed a desire to go dress shopping with me, like it was all part of the ritual of getting married. Amanda too, but I was trying not to think of her today.

"You know," Sylvia said with a sly grin. "You can always go dress shopping back home. Pretend you don't have a dress yet. Then let them know later that you found one."

"You mean lie to them?" I was shocked. Not about the lying, but that Sylvia suggested it.

"A small white lie to save your mom's feelings." Sylvia shrugged. "It's what I'd do. Because you're going to find when planning a wedding that it is virtually impossible to please everyone."

Amanda immediately sprang to mind. "Tell me about it," I muttered under my breath.

My euphoria at finding the dress faded when we picked up the developed film. The clerk handed me the envelope with the prints and told me to have a nice day, and my earlier excitement morphed into something darker and more foreboding. Trepidation. This was it. This was what potentially got Joyce killed.

I looked at Sylvia, who was watching me expectantly.

"Well?" she prompted. "Open it."

Moving away from the counter, I opened the flap and pulled out the prints. Sylvia pressed against my side so she could see as I flipped through them. A photographer, Joyce was not. There were three photos of Sally and Hazel with their heads chopped off. There was a random shot of what I presumed to be Joyce's living room floor. A few shots of the golf course that weren't too bad. And the money shot? Or what I presumed to be the money shot? I couldn't help it. I barked out a laugh, then snorted, quickly slapping a hand over my mouth at the sound.

"What?" Sylvia looked at me, puzzled. "What is it?"

"This." I held the print up to her face. "See this blurry photo? The one of what appears to be someone in a yellow dress? Who's not only blurry but half out of shot? I think that's the photo."

Sylvia plucked it from my fingers and studied it closely. "Are you sure?" She squinted at me.

I flipped through the photographs again. There were no others that matched, and this one was the last in the batch. The last picture Joyce had ever taken—because she'd given her camera to Sally for safekeeping. And it was out of focus with no way of identifying who was in the photo. Joyce had been in a hurry when she took it, not taking time to focus or position the shot, for if she had, she'd have known that Paul was almost entirely out of frame. All we could see of him was from the waist down. The rest of the photo was of Ethel's carpet.

"If this is all Joyce had on him," I said, sliding the

pictures back into the envelope, "then his job is safe."

"But he doesn't—didn't—know that. He saw her take the picture. Otherwise, he'd never have gone along with her feeble blackmail attempts."

"There's something else." I was talking more to myself than to Sylvia, thoughts jumbling and whirling through my mind as I tried to piece the puzzle together. "Joyce told me, when we were out on the green, that Paul was sleeping with the HR Manager, Hayden."

"Really? I didn't get that vibe."

"Me either. But while Kade and your husband are hunting down CCTV footage, I'm going to talk to Hayden, see what she can tell me about Paul."

CHAPTER THIRTEEN

I arrived at the Torres Place admin offices and was greeted by Hayden, the HR Manager. She had a wide smile and a friendly tone, but something about her seemed off, and I couldn't quite put my finger on it.

"Hey, Audrey!" she said. "I'm glad you're here. We didn't meet under the best of circumstances yesterday, so when you called, I figured it would let me make it up to you. I'll show you around."

As we walked through the halls, I observed her carefully. She was a tall woman with long red hair and green eyes. She wore a green silk blouse and a black pencil skirt, which accentuated her curves. But what caught my attention the most was the way she walked—with a confident strut, as if she owned the place.

"So, Hayden," I said, trying to start a conversation. "How long have you been working here?"

"Oh, a few years now," she said. "It's a great job, really. I get to interact with all the residents and make sure they're happy."

"Right," I said, trying to sound casual. "And what's your relationship with Paul Wilson? He's your manager, right?"

Hayden's smile faltered for a second, but then she recovered. "Paul? Oh, we have a good working relationship. He's a great boss."

"I see." I was not convinced. "And you two are just colleagues, right? Nothing more?"

Hayden looked at me with a raised eyebrow. "What do you mean?"

"Well, I heard some rumors that you and Paul were sleeping together," I said, trying to sound nonchalant.

Hayden's expression turned from confusion to anger. "What? Who told you that? That's ridiculous!"

"Just a rumor I heard," I said.

. . .

"I bet it was Sally and Hazel." Hayden scoffed. "They've been spreading lies and gossip ever since they moved in here. You can't believe anything they say."

"Nevertheless," I plowed on, offering up a silent apology to Sally and Hazel for dropping them in it. "They seem pretty convinced that you and Paul were having an affair."

Hayden sighed. "Fine. Yes, Paul and I were seeing each other for a while. But it's over now. We ended things a few months ago."

I was taken aback that she caved so easily. One minute she was angry and offended at the mere notion of an affair, the next she was admitting it.

"I see," I said, trying to refrain from fist pumping the air. "And why did you break up?"

"It just wasn't working out," Hayden said, looking away. "We're better off as friends."

I nodded, pretending to believe her. But something still didn't add up. If Hayden and Paul were really lovers, why did he look at her with such disdain? Maybe the amicable breakup wasn't so amicable after all. Did Hayden find out about his penchant for wearing women's clothes and things had gone south soon after, leaving Paul bitter and jaded?

As if on cue, Paul appeared around the corner, his face twisted in a scowl. "Hayden," he said, his voice dripping with venom. "I need to talk to you in my office. Now."

Hayden looked at me with a worried expression before following Paul down the hall. Naturally, I followed, keen to eavesdrop.

"What the hell were you thinking?" Paul hissed. "Telling her about us? You know how dangerous that is."

"I'm sorry, Paul," Hayden said, her voice shaking. "I didn't mean to—"

"Save it," Paul snapped. "You've put both of us at risk. And if that woman finds out the truth, we're both screwed."

My heart raced as I listened to their conversation. What truth? What were they hiding? Had they killed Joyce? While I tried to make sense of it all, Hayden stormed out of Paul's office, tears streaming down her face. She didn't even notice me standing there.

Paul emerged a moment later, his expression thunderous. He looked at me with cold eyes. "What are you doing here? Poking your nose in where it doesn't belong."

I didn't know how to respond. Part of me wanted to demand answers from him, to accuse him of killing Joyce. But another part of me was wary—worried about what he might do if I pushed him too far. Something more was going on here, and until I got to the bottom of it, I needed to tread carefully.

"I was just leaving," I said, backing away slowly.

Paul didn't say anything else. He just watched me with that cold, calculating gaze as I walked away.

Standing in the elevator, I jabbed the button to the sixth floor like I was hitting the emergency stop on a ride with no brakes. I needed to speak to Joyce, and my best guess was that she was hanging out with either Sally or Hazel, or in her own apartment.

I was right; I found Joyce in her apartment, sitting in her armchair and watching television. If the television had been on, which it wasn't. So, instead, she was sitting watching a blank screen. It was kinda sad. "Hello, Audrey," she said with a smile. "What brings you by?"

"I need you to tell me about Hayden and Paul and what you know of their affair." Because what I witnessed today wasn't adding up. Hayden initially appeared to be a strong and confident woman, yet she'd rushed out of Paul's office in tears moments later, a total one-eighty. Her behavior was... odd. Not to mention Paul's anger and the secret they were keeping had me burning with curiosity.

"Of course, dear," Joyce said. "What do you need?"

I took a deep breath. "I need to know what Hayden and Paul were involved in. I know you were blackmailing Paul with that photo, which, by the way, wasn't the money shot you thought it was. I'm surprised he didn't demand to see proof of it before giving in to your blackmail."

Joyce's expression turned serious. "They were an odd couple, Hayden and Paul. I never really understood their romance."

"What do you mean?"

"One day, you'd stumble across them in the garden or tucked away in a corner somewhere whispering to each other and looking into each other's eyes, sometimes even singing together. The next, they'd be arguing. Always so dramatic and, oh, I don't know, what's the word? Flamboyant?"

"Singing?" My eyebrows shot up. I couldn't imagine Paul Wilson singing. He seemed an angry man, one more prone to shouting and punching walls. Not singing. But then Joyce had found him wearing women's clothing, so clearly, he was a well that ran deep.

Joyce ignored me. "But always, always, they seemed so furtive. Which is why I figured they were having an affair and keeping it secret was paramount."

An idea started to take shape. Probably a bad idea, but now the seed had been planted, I was powerless to resist. "Joyce, I need a favor."

"Of course, dear. What is it?"

"I need you to be my lookout."

"Lookout?" She scratched her head, puzzled.

"I need to get into Paul's office."

"Oh." She nodded. "A little B&E. Not a problem. I'm your gal."

I loved how she was immediately on board with my shady plan. If Joyce were younger—and alive—I could see us being great friends. As it was, she was neither of those things and the clock was ticking. I needed to solve her murder so she could move on, or risk being stuck here, potentially forever.

Retracing my steps, I returned to the administrative offices, casually leaning against the wall and doing my best to appear nonchalant while holding my phone to my ear. "Right," I said to Joyce, keeping my voice low. "I need you to check if Paul is in his office."

"On it." Joyce darted down the hall, occasionally

stopping to press her back against the wall and snap her neck, first one way, then the other, as if keeping a lookout, as if she were in danger of being discovered. I lowered my head and tried not to laugh. Once she was opposite Paul's door, she half crouched, then bolted inside at a running leap. Lord only knew what she thought she was doing. Several minutes passed, and I began to wonder if she'd forgotten her mission when she leaped back out into the hallway and waved at me. Cupping her hands around her mouth, she yelled, "All clear!"

Sliding my phone into my pocket, I hurried down the hall, wrapped my fingers around the doorknob to Paul Wilson's office, and turned. Thankfully, it was unlocked, although I could pick the lock if I needed to. But much easier—and infinitely quicker—to have it already open. Stepping inside, I closed the door behind me as quietly as possible.

"Right," I said, keeping my voice low in case anyone wandering past overheard. "I need you to keep a lookout. Let me know if anyone comes."

"On it." Joyce gave me a mock salute and stepped through the door, while I got busy searching through the papers on Paul's desk. Folders with financial reports, minutes from board meetings, and a hamburger wrapper were piled on top of a paper diary. Opening the diary, I idly flicked through. Nothing very exciting. His appointments revolved around the running of Torres Place, except for two evening appointments where he'd scrawled the word *reverse*.

"What does reverse mean?" Was he having driving lessons? Some past life regression therapy? Every Monday and Thursday evening, for an hour, Paul attended something called reverse. I'd just put the diary down and opened the top drawer when a sound at the door alerted me that someone was there. My eyes widened, watching the doorknob turn. Without a second to spare, I ducked down and crawled under the desk, grateful it was one with a backing that hid the occupant's legs. Sitting on the floor, I pulled my knees to my chest and wrapped my arms around them, holding on tight.

"Oh, shoot!" I heard Joyce gasp. Then she was behind Paul's desk, leaning down and peering at me. "Sorry, he slipped past without me noticing." How that was possible, I didn't know, but I shook my head and held a finger up to my lips.

"Audrey! You need to get out of here. Now!" Joyce

practically screamed. I shook my head again. It was too late, for Paul was already in the room, his footsteps coming toward the desk. If he sat down, I was busted. I held my breath while Joyce danced some sort of Irish jig and appeared to be attempting to shoo Paul away. If I wasn't scared of being discovered, I would have laughed.

"Ah, there it is." He stopped by the desk, his feet mere inches from where I was crouched. I heard shuffling above me, imagined him sorting through the files.

"What's he doing?" I mouthed at Joyce.

"Huh?" She frowned.

"What. Is. He. Doing?" I tried again.

"The weather?" She turned to look out the window. "It's a lovely, fine day. Why? What does that have to do with anything?"

I clamped my lips together and pointed above me. "What is he doing?"

"Oooooh! What's he doing?"

I nodded.

She moved closer until she was partially standing in the desk. "He's picked up a file called Occult Health and Safety."

I snorted, then slapped a hand over my mouth to stifle the sound.

"It's okay," Joyce said. "He didn't hear you. Or if he did, he didn't realize it came from under his desk. You know," she continued on, "I didn't know they had meetings about the Occult here. How interesting. I wonder if it's only for staff or if residents can come along."

"Right," Paul said, then spun on his heel and left the office, the door clicking closed behind him. I waited a few seconds before crawling out.

"Not occult," I said to Joyce, gripping the edge of the desk and hauling myself to my feet. "Occ health and safety. Short for occupational."

"Oh. That doesn't sound anywhere near as interesting."

"Believe me, it isn't." I unfurled my protesting body, accidentally knocking the wastepaper basket over as I did so. "Oops."

I swear every vertebra in my spine cracked as I bent down to pick up the basket and scoop the spilled papers back into it. Most of his rubbish was torn open envelopes, food wrappers, and screwed up post-it notes with reminders of things he had to do. All boring and work related. Until I spotted a bright yellow flyer that had been screwed into a ball.

"Hello, what's this?" I flattened the flyer out, a little taken aback to see the woman on the front, wearing a huge ballgown with her eyes scratched out.

"What is it?" Joyce asked, leaning over my shoulder to see.

"It's a flyer for a performance of *Cinderella* at the Peacock Theater, yet someone—Paul?—has scratched her eyes out."

"Spooky."

"Okay, we need to make this quick, and since you're a lousy lookout, you may as well help me look." I shoved the flyer into my pocket to take with me.

"What are we looking for?"

"Eye drops or nasal spray."

While Joyce stuck her head in the filing cabinet, I quickly went through Paul's drawers. Nothing. No eye drops or nasal spray. Nothing much of a personal nature at all, and I wondered if that was a male thing or just a Paul thing. When I'd worked temp jobs, I'd always take a few personal items with me to brighten up my workspace, but there was none of that in Paul's office. He very much kept his personal life— and personality—out of his office.

We were just about done when my phone started buzzing, announcing a video call from Seb. I hit answer as I headed out of Paul's office and had just glimpsed Seb holding Bandit when I ran smack dab into a hard, immovable object. Staggering backward and trying not to lose my grip on the phone, I looked up into the glaring face of Paul Wilson.

CHAPTER FOURTEEN

"*H*e totally bought it," I hissed as I scurried down the hallway, Paul's glare boring into my back.

"I think he did," Joyce agreed, hustling along beside me.

I'd hung up on Seb, telling him I'd call him back, then lied through my teeth, telling Paul I was searching for my sunglasses that I must have dropped when Hayden had been giving me a tour. He'd snidely pointed out that the tour hadn't included his office, so there was no way I could have dropped them in there, but I'd countered with the theory that someone may have found them and handed them in to Paul. He'd snapped that he wasn't lost and found and then told me to get out. I obliged.

"Now what?" Joyce asked.

"Back to your place." Reaching the elevator, I jabbed the down button, refusing to look over my shoulder to see if Paul was still watching. I suspected he was. An uneasy sensation had the hairs on the back of my neck standing on end, and I figured that was all down to the man glaring at me from down the corridor.

"Oh, good, we can have tea." Joyce smiled, rubbing her hands together, before her smile slipped into a frown. "We've missed *Murder, She Wrote*, though."

"I'm sure there'll be something else you can watch," I assured her, stepping into the elevator. When I turned to face the doors, I caught sight of Paul, spinning on his heel and stalking back into his office. As soon as the elevator doors closed, I let out my breath in a whoosh. That had been closer than I would have liked. One thing was for sure: Ben made a better lookout than Joyce.

"Are you all right, Audrey?"

Straightening my shoulders, I nodded. "I'm fine. That was a close call, that's all. There's something about that man that gives me the creeps."

"Who, Paul? He's harmless."

"So, you don't think he's behind your murder?" I

was shocked. I'd thought Joyce suspected Paul.

"Paul? Goodness, no. He doesn't have the gumption."

"Who do you think killed you?"

She looked at me askance. "I have no idea."

And that's when I felt it. The lie. Joyce Harrison was lying through her teeth. My spidey senses told me so.

"Joyce," I began, trying to keep my voice level. "Who killed you?"

Joyce patted my shoulder, icy shards shooting down my arm and spine, making me shiver. "Sweetheart, I really don't know. Now, why don't we drop it and go have that nice cup of tea, hmm?"

The elevator jolted to a stop at the sixth floor, and before the doors could open, Joyce stepped through them. "This is getting weirder by the minute," I grumbled under my breath, waiting for the doors to open before following Joyce to her apartment.

Once inside, I dutifully turned on the television for Joyce, sniggering at the re-run of *The Golden Girls* that was playing. How apt, for with Joyce, Sally, and Hazel, I felt like we were in a sitcom of our own. I got busy searching the bathroom, then kitchen, rummaging through the trash, searching for eye drops or nasal spray. I found none. Sitting on the kitchen floor, the remnants of Joyce's trash can scattered around me, I had to admit defeat. Whoever doctored Joyce's food either brought it with them and subsequently took it away when they were done, or it wasn't done in her apartment.

My phone started buzzing, Seb's face lighting up the screen, reminding me I said I'd call him back and had completely forgotten.

"Hey, Seb." I smiled brightly, pretending I wasn't sitting on some dead woman's kitchen floor surrounded by garbage. "Sorry, I forgot to call you back."

He waved away my apology. "Don't worry about it. You were obviously busy."

I decided he didn't need to know about my little break and enter and subsequent search of Paul's office. After all, what he didn't know, he couldn't give in evidence.

"Your face is looking... better?" Seb squinted at the screen, bringing the phone closer so he could get a better look.

"Yeah, the swelling has gone down a lot, and the bruising isn't so bad." That's if you liked your eyes a deep shade of purple with green and yellow highlights. "Is everything okay? Bandit? Thor?"

"Relax, they're fine. Missing you, I think."

Behind him I saw a flash of fur, the sounds of paws thundering across wooden floorboards, a slide, and a thud.

"What on earth is going on?"

"Well." Seb squared his shoulders. "Bandit started by stealing my socks. For the life of me, I can't find where she's hidden them. Next, I caught her trying to get into the pantry. Thank goodness you had the foresight to put a lock on that door."

"She is *very* partial to Cheez-its." Hence why I'd had to lock the pantry door. Bandit was, as the name suggested, very good at stealing things.

"Mom?" Bandit called in the background, then more thundering footsteps before she barreled into Seb, practically knocking him off his seat on the couch. He made a garbled *oof* noise before righting himself.

"Relax, she's right here," he said to Bandit, adjusting himself so she could sit on his lap.

"Is she?" I peered closer. "Is she wearing socks?"

"What?" Seb glanced down at the raccoon in his lap, then threw back his head, laughing. "There they are!"

"Bandit." I chuckled. "Why are you wearing Seb's socks?"

"Because I'm being *sneaky*," she stage-whispered. "And Thor told me my claws make too much noise on the floor and that Seb'll hear me."

"Seb will hear you do what?"

She opened her mouth to answer, then paused, head cocked. "I can't remember."

"Snitch," Thor growled, just out of view of the camera. "Have I taught you nothing?"

"You taught me that wearing socks makes my paws slide on the floor and it's fun!" Bandit declared, jumping from Seb's lap to demonstrate as she shot across the floor in the background, sliding until she hit the kitchen counter with a thud.

I burst out laughing.

"How's the investigation coming?" Seb asked.

I glanced down at my surroundings, the rubbish, the impossible task of trying to find the eye drops that had killed Joyce. "It's not." I sighed. "If only I could find the murder weapon."

"Which is? A knife? Gun?"

"Eye drops. Or nasal spray." But more likely it was eye drops. I'd done some research, and it turned out death by eye drops was more common than I ever thought. Who knew? Certainly not me.

"Really?"

I recognized the skepticism on Seb's face, for I'd

worn that expression many times myself. "I know. It's crazy, right? That you can kill someone by emptying a bottle of eye drops into their food or drink."

"A crime of opportunity?"

"What, you think the killer was carrying around a bottle of Visine on the off chance they'd run into Joyce and the perfect opportunity presented itself?" It was so farfetched it just might be plausible. Joyce and her friends frequently dined at the Sunset Café. If ever there was an opportunity to drug someone's food, it would be in a busy café. Walk past, bump into the server, a quick sleight of hand, and job done.

I began scooping up the garbage I was sitting amongst and shoving it back in the bin, the hamster on its wheel that was my brain doing double time.

"What on earth are you doing?" Seb asked. "Is that... garbage?"

"Where?" Thor was immediately interested, and I paused long enough to see his gray, furry face fill the screen.

"Hey, Thor." I smiled, wiping the back of my hand across my forehead. "Are you being good for Seb? Not tricking Bandit into breaking into the pantry or anything?"

His orange eyes narrowed. "Would I do such a thing?"

"Most definitely. Why don't you go put on some socks and slide around on the floor?"

He lifted his head into the air, as if the very thought of such shenanigans was beneath him. Then he looked at me with *Puss in Boots* eyes and I melted. "I miss you," he said. "When are you coming home?"

"Not tomorrow, but the day after. It'll go in a flash, you'll see."

"You know he's not feeding me, right?" His scowl was back, making me laugh.

"He is feeding you. You're on a diet, remember? Just because you can see the bottom of your bowl occasionally doesn't mean there's no food in it."

"What's he saying?" Seb demanded. "Is he complaining I'm not feeding him? God, Audrey, you should hear your cat in the morning. The wailing, like he's been held in captivity, beaten and starved, for days. The drama. You should get an agent for him. He'd do great in movies or television."

Seb wasn't wrong. I knew exactly the type of theatrics he was referring to. "Maybe he was an actor in a previous life?" I suggested.

"Either that or he's going to be one in his next life. Anyway, I was calling to let you know Amanda dropped by—" I opened my mouth, a string of curses poised on the tip of my tongue, but Seb cut me off. "And before you rip her a new one, she came by to collect the cakes. Which turned out quite fortuitous, actually. I got to have a little tête-à-tête with her and explain that while you—we—appreciated her enthusiasm about the wedding, it was, in fact, *your* wedding, *not* hers, and if you wanted to get married in jeans and a tee on the beach at midnight, well that was your choice and she had to butt out."

I sighed wistfully. "Jeans and a tee on the beach at midnight sounds pretty good. And? How did she take it? What did she say?" I was so over the drama that was my sister-in-law. Kade was right. We needed a family meeting where we reminded everyone that while I, the youngest between my brother, sister, and I, and therefore the baby of the family, was actually a grown ass adult, a woman in her thirties who could take care of herself.

"I thought she seemed a tad embarrassed, if I'm honest," Seb surprised me by saying. "Like... sheepish almost."

I snorted at the almost part. Amanda was a gorgeous, stylish, confident woman who walked through life owning it. I couldn't imagine her ever appearing sheepish or contrite. It wasn't in her DNA.

"Doubtful, but thank you, and I'm sorry you got dragged into all this drama."

"Girl"—Seb waved a hand in dismissal—"I'm not only a schoolteacher, but I'm gay. I live for drama. Don't you worry your pretty little head about it." The last was said in a fake southern drawl that made me laugh. "But anyway," he continued on, not giving me time to speak, "you know we missed the bridal expo in the city? Well, the good news, a watered-down version is coming to Firefly Bay, and I've got us tickets."

"Us?"

"You, me—of course—your mom, Laura, and"— he paused for dramatic effect—"Amanda."

"Yay." I could one hundred percent contain my enthusiasm because I had none. I cringed at the mere thought of a bridal expo.

"And the good thing about expos, besides getting to see all the tulle and sparkles, is discounts."

"Discounts?"

"Uh-huh. Book on the day, get a discount. I'm thinking photographer, flowers. Not the venue cos obviously that needs to be booked way in advance, but if you're still set on a summer wedding?"

"I honestly don't care," I confessed. "Fall would work too. Like you said, I'm happy to plan it around when we can book the venue. Do we have a venue?"

"I'm going out this afternoon to tour that converted barn everyone's been raving about. The Harvest Moon."

"A barn?" I mean, I knew I wanted low key and casual, but a barn? Stinking of animal poo and wearing mud boots at the reception wasn't exactly what I had in mind.

"Converted barn," Seb corrected me. "As in, converted to be an entertainment venue for hire. With flushing toilets and everything. Trust me, if I don't think you'll love it, I'll keep searching until I find you the perfect place."

"Thanks, Seb. I know I've said it before, but I'll say it again—I'd be lost without you."

"Darl." He fluttered his eyelashes and ramped up his campiness one thousand percent. "It's my honest to God pleasure."

My phone beeped, and an incoming message from Kade telling me to meet him at the café flashed across my screen.

"Gotta go, Seb. I think Kade's got a lead."

"Mystery and intrigue are afoot! Farewell." After an exaggerated bow, Seb hung up, and I cleaned up Joyce's kitchen before heading to the Sunset Café.

CHAPTER FIFTEEN

I spied Dennis, Sylvia, and Kade sitting at a table out on the terrace. They looked up when I approached, so naturally, I tripped over nothing, staggering the rest of the way.

"Did you tell him?" I asked Sylvia.

"Tell me what?" Kade asked curiously.

Sylvia shook her head. "Nope, that's your bit of news to share. I did tell them the photo Joyce took of Paul was a bust."

I sat down next to Kade and grabbed his hand. "I found a dress!" I could barely contain my relief. "It's perfect."

"A dress? As in... a wedding dress?" He sounded, dare I say, hopeful?

I nodded, my face breaking into a smile that hurt my cheeks.

"Babe, that's fantastic! But... how? You found a dress at the camera store?"

I laughed. "No, silly. While we were waiting for the film to be developed, your mom and I visited a little bridal boutique a couple of doors down, and there it was."

Kade leaned down and kissed me, long and hard. "I'm happy that you're happy."

I leaned back, feeling like a weight had been lifted from my shoulders. I had a dress. I was excited about the dress. Life was good. Now to get down to the business of solving Joyce's murder.

"Have you managed to get a look at the CCTV?" I jerked my head toward the cameras discreetly and strategically placed around the café.

Dennis folded his arms across his chest, a scowl on his face. "They used words like search warrant," he grumbled.

I looked from Kade to his father expectantly. Surely, they'd found their way around the search warrant issue? Only it seemed they hadn't, for both men sat there silently—or in Dennis's case, not so silently—stewing on it.

I sighed and shook my head. "Leave it with me."

"What are you going to do?" Dennis looked at me sharply.

"Audrey," Kade cautioned. "Remember, we're police officers."

"You two might be. I'm not." And sometimes, not being a cop held a lot more sway than having a shiny badge.

"Audrey." Kade pinned me with a look that I shrugged off.

"What?" I said defensively. "You two have been on this since yesterday, and you still haven't gotten your hands on the footage. Time to let me try."

"Can she do that?" Dennis blinked.

"She's not bound by the same rules we are."

"Darn straight I'm not. Watch and learn boys, watch and learn." I made my way to the counter with a certain swagger, concentrating fiercely on not tripping. Leaning one elbow on the counter, I caught the eye of the server, the same man who'd been on duty yesterday morning.

"Hi, there. What can I get you?" His smile was bright, reminding me a little of Seb and his impossibly white teeth. I dropped my eyes to his name badge.

"Hi, Liam, my name's Audrey, and I'm looking into something that happened here yesterday. I'd love to chat with you if you have a few minutes."

He cocked his head. "Didn't I see you in here yesterday? You with those cops?" His gaze landed on the Galloways' table out on the terrace.

"I'm not a cop if that's what's got you worried." I smiled, keeping my tone friendly. "But my fiancé is. And his dad. Well, his dad is retired, but you know..." I trailed off.

"Once a cop, always a cop," Liam said, wiping down the counter. "Look, you're going to have to order something. If the boss sees me chit chatting, he's going to dock my pay."

"Oh! Right, sure." I straightened from my slouch against the counter and perused the menu. "Give me an iced cappuccino with a shot of espresso."

"Coming right up."

While Liam busied himself making my order, he said, "I take it you want to know about Joyce? I don't know what else to tell you, man. She comes in regularly with Sally and Hazel. They had breakfast together yesterday morning, then went out for a round of golf."

"I'm sure you've heard the gossip by now, right? I'm trying to get to the bottom of it."

He paused and eyeballed me. "That she was murdered?" He snorted. "Sure." His tone told me he didn't believe Joyce was murdered, not for a second.

"I'm just trying to find out what happened here. Do you think you could help me out?"

"What do you need?"

"Would it be too much trouble to ask if I could take a peek at the CCTV footage?"

His eyes narrowed. "Don't you need a warrant for that?"

I shook my head. "I'm not a cop. So, no, this is just between us. You're not going to get in trouble." I hesitated, then winked. "Unless you slipped a little something into Joyce's drink, then you might be."

His jaw dropped. "You think Joyce was *poisoned*?"

I shrugged. "Like I said, just trying to get to the bottom of it."

Liam considered his options for all of two nano seconds before caving. "Okay, fine. But don't tell my boss."

"Or he'll dock your pay." I crossed my heart. "Promise I won't tell him."

Liam leaned down and pulled a tablet from beneath the counter, his fingers swiping across the screen, punching in a pin number or password or something before he held it out to me. "Here. Here's the footage from yesterday."

"Thank you."

There were three cameras in the café—one directed at the counter, one that covered the main café and the door leading into the interior of the Torres Place building, and another outside focused on the terrace.

I chose the one trained on the tables inside and hit play, watching on the screen as Liam set up in the morning, preparing to open. "What happens to the footage?" I asked, speeding up the replay and sending Liam into double time on the screen. "Does it get deleted? Saved in the cloud?"

"Dunno." Liam slid my drink toward me. "That'll be five dollars."

"Thanks." I paid, adding a generous tip, and took a sip while watching the footage, slowing it down when I got to the part where Joyce arrived with Hazel and Sally. It was surreal watching them on the screen. I switched cameras, following the women outside to the terrace.

"Joyce had orange juice and scrambled eggs."

"That's right. Her usual order. That woman loved her eggs," Liam said. I'd forgotten he was there, so when he spoke, I jumped, spilling my drink.

"Oh shoot, sorry," I muttered, blindly feeling around for a napkin, unable to drag my eyes off the screen. Something had to have happened in the café. I didn't want to miss it.

"Get your fingers out of it," Liam admonished, shoving my hand away. "I'll clean it up."

On the screen, two paramedics arrived. Both male. Both waved at the women sitting at Joyce's table, then headed to the counter to place their order. They kept their backs to the camera, so I couldn't get a good look at their faces, but they didn't look like the guys who'd arrived to collect Joyce's body. I was eighty percent certain they were different builds, although it was hard to tell from the back and with them wearing uniforms.

"Liam, who are these guys?" I showed him the tablet.

"Uh, they're paramedics, Audrey." He made me sound like I was an idiot for not knowing that.

"No, I mean, do you know who they are personally? They waved at Joyce, Hazel, and Sally."

"Oh, yeah, I think they know them?" Liam squinted and pointed at the screen. "That one ordered them a round of drinks."

"Wow. That was nice of him."

"Guess they're just nice guys." Liam shrugged,

not thinking much of it. "Those guys are always getting called out here. Half the time, it's a false alarm. Like they have to do those assessment things when someone has a fall?"

"So, I'm guessing they probably know a lot of the residents."

"For sure." Liam looked over my shoulder. "They probably know every single person in here. Bar you."

"Thanks," I muttered under my breath, switching cameras, searching for the same footage from a different angle. Eventually I found it, fast forwarding the camera that covered the counter until I got to the two paramedics. Still not an incredibly clear shot, the camera was focused on the staff behind the counter, not the customers. Both paramedics were side on, neither of them moving to face the camera directly.

As surreptitiously as possible, I pulled out my phone and snapped a photo, then continued watching the footage from the main café camera. The paramedics collected their order. One of them snatched up a napkin, wiped the counter where his cup had been, then tossed it in the trash on the way out.

"Anything?" Liam asked.

I shook my head. "Do you suffer from allergies?"

He appeared surprised by the question. "No. Why?"

"So, you don't use a nasal spray or eye drops?"

"No, and even if I had allergies, I'd just pop an antihistamine."

"Good point." I handed back the tablet. "Thanks, Liam, I appreciate you helping out."

"So?" He took the tablet and placed it back under the counter. "Did you see who killed her?"

I sighed, shoulders slumping, and finished my drink. "I did not. No one approached their table other than the wait staff, delivering their meals."

"You think one of us did it?"

"Did you?"

"I already told you I didn't." He frowned. "Do you think it was Chef?"

"You mean your chef? The one who prepares the meals at the café?"

"No. Well, yes, but we legit call him Chef. It's his nickname. But he's also the cook, yes."

"Right... so did Chef have a beef with the ladies? With Joyce? He'd know their orders right, seeing as they're regulars?"

"Chef doesn't have a beef with anyone. He's one of those perpetually friendly people, always cheerful. Even if a customer is chewing him out, he'll smile and apologize and get on with his day with no hard feelings."

"He's no Gordon Ramsey then?"

"Polar opposite."

"Would I be pushing the friendship if I asked to look around the kitchen?" I lowered my head and looked up at him through my lashes. I was aiming for cute and adorable but probably came across as manic and slightly unhinged, given the bruised state of my face.

"No can do. Staff only. There's no way I can get you in there." But he was giving me this look. One I couldn't decipher. For while his words were saying no, his eyes were saying yes.

I cast my mind around frantically, trying to decipher what Liam wasn't saying. "That's too bad, Liam," I said with exaggerated calmness. "I would have liked to see your setup back there."

"Chef goes on break from two till four. That's a really bad time to visit."

"Two till four, huh? What happens then... to the menu, I mean?"

"No hot food. We have pre-prepared sandwiches and croissants. I can heat a quiche in the microwave. But it's quiche. In the microwave."

"I hear ya. Well, thanks, Liam. That was the best

coffee I've had all day." Giving him a salute, I ambled back out to the terrace. If he meant what I thought he'd meant, I should get my butt back here sometime between two and four for a sneaky poke around in the kitchen.

CHAPTER SIXTEEN

"It's a long shot," Dennis said. He'd been a little put out when I'd returned to the table victorious, having succeeded where he'd failed.

"One hundred percent." It was definitely a long shot. I'd been hoping to get footage of Paul Wilson in the café that morning, but he hadn't arrived until after Joyce's body had been found. If he was the killer, and I was definitely thinking he was, then he'd poisoned her somewhere else. I just needed to find out where. I doubted I'd find anything incriminating in the kitchen, but no stone left unturned and all that.

Reaching into my pocket, I pulled out the scrunched up flyer to the *Cinderella* play I'd found in Paul's trash can.

"What's that you've got there, Audrey?" Sylvia asked.

I handed her the flyer. "I found this in Paul's office."

"You broke into his office?" Kade's eyebrows practically hit his hairline. Trouble with dating a cop is they want you to follow the rules, those pesky little rules otherwise known as the law.

"It wasn't locked, so technically I didn't break in anywhere."

Kade sighed and shook his head, plucking the flyer from his mom's fingers and studying it. "What's the significance?"

"No idea. But the way the eyes have been scratched out had me intrigued."

"You think Paul scratched them out?"

"I think it's a possibility. He seems to be a very angry man."

Dennis took the flyer from Kade and held it at arms' length while he studied the woman. "She looks familiar." He held the flyer toward Sylvia. "Do we know her?"

Sylvia cocked her head. "It's hard to see past the eyes, to focus on her face without seeing the vandalism."

"I know!" Dennis thumped the table, making the

silverware jump and rattle. "She looks like the woman from yesterday, the one who came out with Paul when we found Joyce's body."

"Hayden?" I grabbed the flyer from him. Sylvia was right, it was hard to focus on anything other than the scratched out eyes, but Dennis was also right, the woman on the flyer bore a resemblance to Hayden Lee, only Hayden was a redhead and the woman on the flyer was blonde.

Seeing I wasn't convinced, Sylvia said, "Take away the ballgown and the wig and look at the bone structure, the shape of her jaw, the length of her neck."

"You think this is Hayden, playing the role of Cinderella?" I still couldn't see it. Kade leaned in close, his body pressed against mine as he studied the flyer again.

"You could be right," he eventually said.

"What does it even matter?" I sighed. "It's hardly relevant."

"Ah!" Dennis jabbed a finger at me from across the table, eyes dancing with enthusiasm. He was really enjoying the thrill of the chase. "That's where the answer often lies. In the unexpected. In the little clues that you toss away as irrelevant."

"Are you sure you're not a detective?" I teased.

"I was happy on my beat." He may have been happy as a beat cop, but I didn't miss the way his chest puffed out with pride when I mentioned his detective skills. Like his son, Dennis Galloway would have made a brilliant detective.

"Joyce said she thought Paul and Hayden were having an affair," I said to the table in general. "I visited Hayden today, and she confirmed it was true, but then Paul caught us talking and summoned Hayden to his office where he chewed her out for talking to me. Something about a secret that, if it gets out, will end them. I'm paraphrasing here."

"So, they're sleeping together?" Sylvia's hand went to her throat, and I wasn't sure if she was surprised or horrified. Yeah, I couldn't imagine anyone wanting to sleep with Paul Wilson either.

"Were. She said it only lasted a few weeks."

"What else did Joyce say?" Kade asked.

"That she'd often come across them acting weird around the facility, like tucked away in a little hidey hole, sometimes acting like lovebirds, other times arguing, even singing."

"Singing?" Sylvia muttered, then grabbed my arm, her voice urgent. "I've got it!"

"Is it catching?" Dennis teased, but Sylvia ignored him, her gaze intense.

"Put it all together," she urged me. "Paul Wilson wearing a dress, a flyer for *Cinderella*, Paul and Hayden *acting* oddly. Singing." She paused, then pushed the flyer toward me, pointing. Under the word Cinderella, in smaller print, were the words pantomime.

"Oh my God." I tipped my head back and looked up at the trellis covering the roof of the terrace, laughing. "Of course. Even the entry in his diary makes sense now. It wasn't reverse. It was rehearse. Paul Wilson is an actor in a pantomime—*Cinderella* to be exact—and I'm guessing Hayden is playing the leading role, something that Paul isn't too thrilled about."

"I don't get it," Dennis confessed. "You're saying Paul and Hayden are actors?"

I nodded. "Performers in a pantomime. Maybe Paul coveted the lead role, hence him trying on Ethel's gown. It would also explain the scratched out eyes. He's jealous."

"Yes, but what does it have to do with Joyce's death?" Sylvia asked, tapping her lip.

I deflated like a balloon. "Maybe it doesn't?" I'd been so sure Paul was behind Joyce's murder, but our new theory, the one where he was an actor playing a part in a play, made perfect sense. I just needed to confirm it was true. "Who fancies going to the theater tonight?"

"Dinner and a show sounds wonderful!" Sylvia clapped her hands together in delight. "We have reservations at Etoile, anyway. Let me check the times when *Cinderella* is showing, and I'll get us tickets."

"Looks like we're going to see *Cinderella*, son," Dennis deadpanned.

"Looks like it, Dad."

"Boys," Sylvia admonished, eyeballing the pair of them. "Behave. It'll be nice to go out. Dennis, we're going to Etoile first, your favorite restaurant, so you can quit your grumbling and plaster a smile on your face and at least pretend to enjoy yourself. That goes for you too, Kade."

"Hey," Kade protested, raising his hands as if to fend her off. "I didn't say anything."

"You didn't have to. Your face did all the speaking for you."

As we finished our lunch, my thoughts turned to Joyce and who killed her. I'd yet to find any trace of Visine, which was puzzling because I thought almost everyone on the planet had a bottle of it tucked away in their medicine cabinet. I kept glancing at my watch, eager for two o'clock to roll around so I could go snoop in the kitchen, for I'd convinced myself that was where Joyce had been poisoned and where I'd find the evidence I was seeking.

"What's wrong?" Kade whispered in my ear.

I jumped, a guilty flush heating my cheeks. "What? Nothing!"

"You keep checking the time. Got a date?" he teased. I laughed and leaned into him.

"No, but I don't think you want to know what I have planned."

"Audrey." There it was again. So much emotion and meaning loaded into one word. A warning—whatever you're thinking of doing, don't. Resignation —you're going to do it despite what I think, aren't you? Acceptance—for the love of God, don't get caught. Do I need bail money?

"Babe." I patted his cheek. "It's fine. Why don't you spend some quality time with your parents? I won't be long."

After Kade and his parents left, I had time to kill, so I took a wander around the gardens, taking a moment to enjoy the beautiful surroundings and peace and quiet. I was sitting on a bench seat under a tree when I spied Joyce, walking alongside a younger woman. From the family resemblance, I assumed it was her daughter, Anne.

Joyce saw me and waved, and I automatically raised my arm to return the gesture when I caught Anne's puzzled look.

"Sorry," she said as she approached. "Do I know you?"

"Um, no, sorry. I thought you were someone else." Anne's eyes were bloodshot and puffy and the tip of her nose red, as if she'd been crying. Which no doubt she had because her mother had recently died, I reminded myself. Of course, she was upset.

"Is everything all right?" I asked, then patted the bench next to me. "Would you like to sit?"

To my utter surprise, she did.

"Thank you. I'm Anne."

"Audrey."

A couple of seconds of silence ticked by. "My mother died."

"Oh, that's tough. I'm so sorry for your loss." It was such a trite thing to say, but really, what can you say in situations like that? I couldn't very well blurt out that her dead mother's ghost was there with us, currently admiring the flowers in a nearby garden bed and watching the butterflies as they danced in the air.

"Do your parents live here?" Anne asked, pulling out a tissue and blowing her nose.

"My in-laws recently moved into one of the independent living apartments. We're here to visit for a few days."

"Your in-laws are lovely," Joyce piped up.

"That's nice. So, you're not from Chicago?"

I shook my head. "A little town called Firefly Bay."

"That sounds familiar."

"Oh? You've been to Firefly Bay?"

"No... wasn't it on the news? Something about a corrupt police department. Some investigation and a bunch of cops were arrested?"

"Oh, yeah. That." Not exactly what we'd like Firefly Bay to be remembered for, but if outing the officers who'd forced my best friend Ben out of his career was the result, I was all for it. "Things are much better now."

Anne looked at me, her pale face intrigued. "Did you *know* them?"

Pursing my lips, I nodded. "Sadly, yes. My fiancé is a detective—not one of the corrupt ones," I hastened to add. "But he was part of the investigation, and my best friend was one of the officers on the receiving end of the corrupt cops. He got forced out of a job he loved."

"That's awful!" Joyce cried, straightening from where she'd been trying to touch a flower to look at me.

"That's awful," Anne echoed. "I'm so sorry that happened to your friend. What kind of world are we living in?"

"I know, right?" I sighed. But things had turned out okay for Ben. He'd started Delaney Investigations. He had a gorgeous home, fancy car, and was sitting pretty financially. Until he'd died and left it all to me. I absently watched the butterflies and listened to the birds chirping and couldn't fathom that we were in Chicago, the sounds of traffic and general noise somehow excluded from the enclosed garden. It was a little slice of paradise, and I thought the architects were brilliant with their placement, the way the towering buildings surrounding the garden blocked the noise, yet allowed light.

"I don't know how I'm going to pay for it," Anne whispered, her hands twisting the tissue until it tore.

"Pay for what?" I kept my voice low, sensing that Anne was on the verge of a breakdown. She seemed fragile, as if the slightest breeze would shatter her into a million pieces. My heart hurt for her. I couldn't imagine what it would feel like to lose my mom. To say I'd be devastated wouldn't begin to cover it.

A single tear overflowed and trickled down her cheek.

"I can't pay for my mother's funeral," Anne whispered, closing her eyes and silently sobbing.

"What?" Joyce sat down on the other side of her daughter. "You don't have to worry about that, Anne. I had insurance. It's all paid for."

"You know"—I placed a soothing hand on Anne's shoulder—"sometimes people take out insurance to cover funeral costs. Is there any chance your mom maybe did something like that?"

Anne lifted her head and looked at me. "Insurance?" She sniffed. "She never said."

"In my closet, top shelf, is a folder with all my documents. Will and so forth. It's all there," Joyce said.

"If she had, I'll bet it's with her will." I smiled, doing my best to be reassuring. "Maybe take a look?"

Anne sniffed again. "Thank you. I will." She turned to me, eyes awash with tears. "This is going to sound terrible, and I don't even know you, but I don't know what I'm going to do without my mom."

"I never knew your mom, but from what I hear, she was a great lady."

Anne gulped, wiped her fingers beneath her eyes, and cocked her head. "Wait. How do you know that? How do you know who my mom is?"

Oh, crap. Plastering what I hoped was a comforting smile on my face, I explained, "I'm assuming your mom is Joyce Harrison? She died the day we arrived. Actually, it was us—me, my fiancé, and his parents—who found her."

"Oh, my God, that was you?"

I nodded. "Her friends, Sally and Hazel, told me a little about you."

"They said some lady visiting was investigating her death. They said you thought it was murder!"

"Haven't the police talked to you?"

"I got a call, but I guess I was too distraught to really take in what they said."

Scooping up her hand in mine, I explained. "They found high levels of a drug called tetrahydrozoline in her system. It's typically found in eye drops and nasal sprays."

Anne frowned. "Are you saying someone overdosed my mother with eye drops? How did they administer them? I'm pretty sure she wouldn't have sat there and let someone put drops in her eyes without her permission. And especially not enough to kill her."

"No, no. Tetrahydrozoline is toxic when ingested. Someone put it in her food."

Anne snatched her hand out of mine and looked at me, aghast at the suggestion someone had killed her mother.

"Do you think *I* did it?"

What? How did she jump to that conclusion? We'd gone from explaining her mother hadn't died from natural causes to accusing her of murder in under three seconds.

"Did you?" May as well play devil's advocate. After all, she was the one who brought it up. Although, to be honest, I didn't think Anne had killed her mom. She was genuinely distraught at her passing. Unless that grief was because she'd murdered her own mother? Now I was second guessing myself, never a good sign.

"Audrey!" Joyce admonished. "My daughter didn't kill me."

"I didn't kill my mom," Anne cried. "I loved her. I don't know how I'm going to live without her. She was my best friend and now? Now she's just... gone." The tears were back in full force.

"It's all right, love," Joyce soothed. "I'm still here."

"And it wasn't just the money, though God knows it was embarrassing having to rely on your mother to send you money every week because you couldn't manage on your own." Anne's voice rose, an edge of hysteria creeping in. "But we couldn't pay the bills, you know. They cut off our electricity. If it hadn't been for Mom bailing us out, we'd be sitting in the dark eating cold beans out of a can."

I looked at Joyce, who was trying to comfort her distraught daughter. She glanced over and caught me looking. "What?" she snapped. "Do something. Can't you see she's upset?"

"You sent her money?" I mouthed silently.

"Do I have any honey? Why on earth would I have any honey?"

I shook my head and tried again. "You. Sent. Her. Money?"

"Poo me dentist lorry? You're not making any sense. Are you having a stroke?"

Sighing, I patted Anne's back and said out loud, "Sally told me you're a schoolteacher... aren't you working at the moment?"

Anne sobbed. "I am. And my husband's a paramedic. And you'd think we'd be managing just fine, wouldn't you? Two incomes. Although my salary is a pittance, and if I didn't love the kids so much, I'd give it away and go waitress or something... I'd probably earn more."

"I know what it's like to struggle to make ends meet," I said. It wasn't a lie. I'd lived from paycheck to paycheck for longer than I cared to admit, and if it wasn't for Ben's inheritance, I wouldn't be where I was today. I'd probably be stumbling from one temp job to another with home ownership and tropical vacations a far-off dream.

Anne surged to her feet, wiping her hands across her face. "I've got to go." She took off before I could say anything more, Joyce rushing after her, leaving me to ponder the fact that it appeared Joyce was subsidizing her daughter and son-in-law financially. Motive for murder? Hardly. You wouldn't kill the cash cow, would you?

CHAPTER SEVENTEEN

At two fifteen, I sidled into the café. Liam saw me and promptly picked up a tray and a cloth and headed out to the terrace to clear tables. Inside, the café was empty, the lunch rush over. Two men sat outside, lingering over their drinks, maybe reliving their morning of golf, blow by blow. Or was that putt by putt? Either way, the coast was clear, and I darted behind the counter, crouching low in case someone unexpectedly came in.

The kitchen was tiny. Immaculate but tiny. A quick perusal of the shelves turned up nothing, but then you'd hardly leave your eye drops out in full view in a commercial kitchen. I scoured that room for a solid hour, top to bottom, and turned up absolutely nothing. Even the trash cans were empty.

Liam appeared in the doorway. "Find anything?"

I shook my head. "Nope."

He noticed I had the trash can lid in my hand. "We empty bins twice a day into the dumpster out back."

"When does the dumpster get collected?"

"Every Saturday morning. Look"—Liam checked the time on the wall clock—"maybe you should go? Sometimes Chef comes back early." I knew he was nervous about getting in trouble for letting me back here, so I put the lid back on the bin, dusted my hands on the seat of my jeans, and smiled.

"Thanks for all your help, Liam. You've been a champ. I'll get out of your hair."

He nodded, shifted his weight from one foot to the other, then said, "Will you keep me posted on what you find out? You know, who killed her and all that? I feel invested now."

"Sure." I brushed past him, checked the café was clear, then hurried back to the Galloways' apartment, a plan forming in my head with each step. If what I suspected was true and the eye drops were administered in the café, the killer would have probably ditched the bottle as soon as possible, not wanting to be caught with potential evidence. Meaning they'd likely tossed them in one of the trash cans at the café. Therefore, the empty bottle of eye drops could be languishing in the dumpster as we spoke.

But there wasn't time to search the dumpster right now. Plus, it was daylight. Dumpster diving was definitely an after dark activity if you didn't want to get caught.

"Dare I ask?" Kade greeted as he opened the door and let me in.

"Everything's fine!" I beamed, the muscles pulling tight in my face, sending aftershocks of pain across my cheekbones. "How's my face?" I put a hand to my nose and veered into the bathroom rather than the living room where I'd originally been heading.

"It looks better today," Kade said, watching me from the doorway.

I snorted, copping an eyeful of myself. I looked horrific. I was amazed Anne had even said hello to me, given I looked like I'd been beaten up and dragged through a hedge backward.

"What time is dinner?"

"Six. Mom got us an early reservation."

"And the play?"

"Eight."

Which meant the play wouldn't be finished until

around ten thirty. By the time we got back home, it would probably be eleven, which left me planning a clandestine dumpster diving adventure for midnight.

"Audrey Fitzgerald." Kade sighed. "What are you plotting now? And don't bother trying to deny it. I can see the cogs turning from here."

I tilted my head and fluttered my eyelashes at him, making him laugh.

"I'm not going to like it, am I?" He chuckled.

"Probably not," I agreed. "How do you feel about dumpster diving?"

"As a recreational pastime? Not a fan. Don't see the appeal."

"Right? Gross. But..."

"Is that what you were doing this afternoon?" Kade backed up a step.

"No! Geez, no need to back away. I don't stink of trash." As if to prove it, I sidled up to him and wrapped my arms around his neck. "But I have plans to indulge later tonight. Care to join?"

Settling his hands on my hips, Kade sighed. "If it means keeping you out of trouble, why not?"

I jerked my head back in surprise. I hadn't expected him to say yes. "Really?" My voice came out more hopeful than I would have liked.

"Yes, really." He pressed his forehead against mine. "I realize I've been a bit neglectful of you this trip, leaving you to your own devices maybe a little too long."

"That's okay. This trip was for you to visit with your parents. Anyway, I've been investigating Joyce's murder. It's fine."

"This trip was for both of us to visit with my parents, for them to get to know you and you to get to know them."

My heart skipped a beat, then took off at double time. "Don't they like me?" I whispered, horrified I'd scared them off with my ghost talking abilities and passion for solving mysteries. I wasn't everyone's cup of tea, but I'd thought Sylvia, Dennis, and I were getting along fine. Had I read the whole situation wrong?

"They love you," Kade assured me. "Almost as much as I do, I suspect."

"Oh, thank God, cos I love them too. I think they're great!" I gushed.

"What I'm saying, Audrey, is I'd like to spend a bit of alone time with you, and if the only way to do that is to go dumpster diving, then that's what I'll do."

Wrapping my arms around his waist, I rested my

cheek on his chest and marveled at how lucky I was to land the most incredibly handsome, supportive, emotionally intelligent, sexy man on earth. Who else would go dumpster diving with you just so they could spend time with you?

"I'm so glad I'm marrying you," I whispered.

"Ditto." His lips grazed my ear, sending shivers down my spine. "We have a couple of hours before we need to get ready."

"Uh-huh."

His hands blazed a trail down my back, cupping my butt. "How about we take a nap?"

I smiled, pressing closer. "I could really use a *nap*."

I stepped into Etoile, my arm linked through Kade's, grateful I'd had the foresight to pack a little black dress. It helped that I'd googled the restaurant, and I don't know what made me think we'd end up dining there—women's intuition maybe—but whatever it was, I was extremely grateful for it. I doubt they'd have let me in if I'd turned up in my customary jeans and T-shirt.

Etoile had an elegant ambiance. Soft lighting

and classical music set the mood, and while we waited to be seated, I took in the beautiful décor and the attention to detail that had gone into every aspect of the restaurant. Tables were set with crisp linens and sparkling silverware, with a small vase of fresh flowers sitting in the center.

"It's so lovely," I whispered to Sylvia, who'd dressed for the occasion in a stunning silver sequin number that draped her curves and fell to the floor in soft waves. She'd kept her makeup simple but gone with a bold red lip that I confess I was envious of. For a woman in her early sixties, she looked amazing—and younger than her actual years.

"We like it. Obviously not somewhere we dine every night, but when you want something special, Etoile is it."

We were seated at a table near the back, and I was relieved by the dark lighting that would hopefully hide any mishaps. Given my clumsy gene, fancy restaurants made me very nervous. Hence the black dress, the perfect color should I spill anything on it.

"What do you recommend?" I asked Dennis as I perused the menu, skimming over the delicious array of French cuisine on offer.

"I'm partial to the coq au vin," Dennis said. "And,

of course, you can't go past the crème brûlée. Sadly, Sylvia won't allow me to order a dessert for the main course." He winked at his wife, and she chuckled, leaning back in her chair when the waiter appeared by her side to pour a glass of champagne.

"I hope you don't mind," she said to me and Kade, "but I went ahead and ordered champagne on our arrival."

"Not at all." I watched as the bubbles fizzed and popped in her glass. I could use a little alcoholic fortification. Kade reached under the table and rested his hand on my thigh, giving it a light squeeze.

"Thanks, Mom," Kade said, keeping an eye on proceedings as the waiter made his way around the table filling our glasses.

"I'd like to make a toast," Sylvia declared once he was done. "As a mother, I have always wanted nothing but the best for you, Kade, and seeing you so happy with Audrey fills my heart with joy. I've watched you grow into the man you are today, and I am proud of the love, respect, and commitment you show toward your fiancée. Your journey together is only just beginning, but I know it will be full of love, happiness, and endless possibilities.

"Audrey, I want to welcome you to our family

with open arms. I couldn't be more thrilled to have you as a daughter-in-law. You are a remarkable woman with many talents and qualities, and I know you will make Kade very happy. I wish you both a lifetime of happiness, love, and adventure. Cheers to the happy couple!"

I confess I was a little misty eyed at the unexpected toast and had to blink back tears while I took a sip of champagne, the bubbles tickling my nose. Dennis added his hearty congratulations, and I left it to Kade to thank them on our behalf, for I wasn't sure I could get any words out past the lump in my throat.

After the toast was done and everyone was perusing their menus once more, Kade leaned toward me. "Okay?"

"I'm fine." I smiled and discretely dabbed beneath my eyes with my fingertips. I'd taken extra care with my makeup this evening, not only to hide the bruises, but I'd also wanted to look nice, and the last thing I wanted was tears ruining all my hard work. "Just a little emotional."

"You look beautiful." He kissed my cheek, then entwined his fingers with mine. Sylvia watched on with a satisfied grin curling her lips. She winked at me, then turned her attention to the waiter, who was poised and ready to take her order.

"You know, I think I'll start with the quiche with bouillabaisse, and like Dennis said, you can't go past the crème brûlée for dessert," she said.

"Very good, madame. And for you, sir?" I noticed the waiter hadn't written anything down and marveled he could remember not only Sylvia's order, but the entire table. Now that took skill, and I was impressed.

After Dennis had ordered, it was my turn. I went with lyonnaise salad, beef bourguignon, and the crème brûlée because I sensed the table would revolt if I did not.

When the food arrived, it looked beautiful, and I was struck by how colorful and intricate my salad was. It put my efforts of throwing together a handful of lettuce leaves and chopped tomatoes to shame.

Conversation and champagne flowed, and by the time we'd finished our meals, my head was buzzing, and I felt quite giddy. It was probably a good thing we were about to sit through a two-and-a-half-hour play. It'd give me a chance to sober up. I couldn't imagine searching the dumpster later tonight in this condition.

Sylvia and Dennis insisted on paying, with Kade

and I protesting the entire time. Five-star restaurants were not cheap, and it wasn't as if we couldn't afford it. However, eventually, we had to admit defeat when Dennis slapped his credit card down and declared dinner a roaring success.

After a quick refresh in the bathroom, we hailed a cab, and it was on to the Peacock Theater for the *Cinderella* pantomime. Sylvia had gotten us front row tickets, and as we waited for the play to start, I flicked through the program I'd picked up in the foyer.

"Oh, lordy, lordy, lordy," I whispered, eyes widening. Inside was a picture of an actor playing one of the ugly sisters. The first thing that caught my eye was the over-the-top costume. The dress was bright pink, almost neon, with layers upon layers of ruffles and frills. It was so big it looked like it would take up an entire row of seats in the theater.

But it was the actor's face that really captured my attention. They were wearing a thick layer of makeup, which exaggerated their features to create a comically grotesque appearance. Their nose was bulbous and red, and their eyebrows were arched so high they almost reached their hairline. But it was their mouth that really stole the show. The actor had managed to contort their lips into a twisted grimace, with their teeth bared in a way that was simultaneously hilarious and unsettling.

Despite the exaggerated makeup and costume, the actor's eyes told a different story. Even though they were playing a character who was supposed to be mean and cruel, there was a glint of humor and mischief in their gaze. It was as if they were in on the joke, having just as much fun as the audience. They were the eyes of Paul Wilson.

"What?" Kade whispered, throwing his arm around my shoulders and pulling me into his side for a cuddle.

"This"—I jabbed at the program on my lap—"is Paul Wilson. He's playing the role of one of the ugly stepsisters."

"No way." Kade plucked the program from my fingers and held it up, squinting in the dim lighting of the theater. "Holy cow. You're right. It says so right here. Stepsister number two played by Paul Wilson."

I snatched the program back and flicked through the pages until I came to the center spread. And there she was, Cinderella, stunning in her gown and glass slippers. Hayden Lee.

Kade and I exchanged a look, my mind racing with questions. Was this the big secret Paul was so desperate to keep hidden? The one he'd ripped into

Hayden about? But why? So what that they were in a play together? Or was it the fact that Paul was playing the part of a woman? But that wasn't unheard of, especially in a pantomime.

"None of this makes any sense," I muttered, grinding my teeth.

The lights dimmed, and the murmur of the audience died down to a low hum. The curtains parted, and the stage came to life, revealing a magical world of fairy tales and enchantment.

The set was a wonderland of glittering castles, lush forests, and twinkling stars, transporting us to a world far, far away. The orchestra began to play, and the familiar tune of *A Dream Is a Wish Your Heart Makes* filled the theater, sending shivers down my spine.

Suddenly, the scene changed, and the stage was filled with colorful characters, each one more dazzling than the last. Cinderella herself appeared, her beautiful gown sparkling under the stage lights. My eyes widened in wonder as the story unfolded before me. I forgot Paul Wilson and Hayden Lee, for I was immersed in a fairytale world of make-believe, transported to a world of romance and fantasy.

As the play drew to a close, the audience erupted into thunderous applause, and I turned to Kade. "Do you think Paul is trying to keep his acting hobby a secret?" I whispered.

Kade's eyes widened in surprise, and he leaned in closer. "What do you mean?"

"I mean, he was trying on Ethel's dress—a costume from her Broadway days. Joyce said she saw him with Hayden, frequently, and sometimes they were singing. I don't think they were having an affair at all. I think they were rehearsing. And I think, as chief operations manager of Torres Place, he's worried about his professional reputation if *this*"—I gestured to the stage—"got out."

CHAPTER EIGHTEEN

*a*s soon as the lights came on, we hustled backstage. It's amazing what the flash of a badge can get you. Kade had put on his cop voice, and the unkempt teenager running around with a clipboard had ushered us through without hesitation.

Backstage was a flurry of activity. Actors hurried to change out of their costumes and makeup, while others were taking down the set and props. The air was filled with chatter, laughter, and the occasional congratulatory hug or handshake.

I followed Kade through the chaos, dodging cables and costumes strewn about, until we reached the dressing room, Sylvia and Dennis hot on my heels. It was packed with actors, each claiming a spot to take off their makeup and change into their regular clothes. It was cramped and hot, but everyone was too caught up in the performance's excitement to care.

As we made our way to Paul's dressing station, I caught glimpses of other actors, some still in their elaborate costumes, others already in casual clothes. There was a sense of camaraderie there, a shared bond among those who had just put on a show for an audience.

I heard snippets of conversations, actors discussing their performances, exchanging compliments and feedback. Others were already making plans for the after-party or discussing their next projects. Despite the exhaustion that comes after a performance, there was an undeniable energy filling the room.

Paul was already in street clothes, sitting at a dressing table, wiping the heavy stage makeup from his face. He saw us coming in the mirror and froze, half rising, before a flash of resignation had him lowering himself back down again.

"I see you put it together," he said, eyes meeting mine in the mirror.

"Great play," I offered. "You and Hayden did a brilliant job."

"Thanks." He didn't appear excited about my praise.

"Why the secrecy? This is what all that sneaking around was about, right? You and Hayden weren't really having an affair."

He snorted out a laugh. "No. We weren't." His tone told me the mere thought of sleeping with Hayden was on par with stepping in dog doo doo. Good to know my intuition hadn't been wrong—despite what Joyce had told me, and what Hayden had confessed, I'd been certain Paul was not romantically attracted to Hayden in the slightest.

"Why the lies?"

"You think the board would approve of this?" His voice went up a couple of octaves as he waved his hand around the dressing room. "They're a bunch of old school, homophobic morons caught up in old-fashioned ideals."

"You think they'd fire you for acting in a play?" Sylvia sounded as shocked as I felt.

"Hell, you brought *them* with you?" Paul snapped, glaring at me.

"We're not going to tell anyone if that's what you're worried about," Sylvia huffed. "But if you're so scared about being found out, why do it at all?"

"Excellent question," I said to her, then turned to

Paul. "Well? If it's so detrimental to your career—which, FYI, I don't think it is. There are unfair dismissal laws to protect you from this sort of thing—why risk doing it at all?"

"I've always loved the theater. As a child, I'd put on plays in the backyard, casting myself in the starring role, of course. I continued to pursue my passion for acting through high school and college, participating in school productions, and taking acting classes.

"But as I got older, I realized my love of acting would never be enough to support me financially. I knew that the odds of making it as a full-time actor were slim, and I didn't want to struggle to make ends meet. So, I pursued a more practical career path and went to business school.

"After years of hard work and dedication, I became the COM of Torres Place, and don't get me wrong, I love my job and I'm good at it, but I never lost my love of acting. When I saw an ad in the paper that they were casting for *Cinderella*, I jumped at the chance to audition.

"Imagine my surprise when I was cast as one of the ugly stepsisters. I admit, at first, I was disappointed—after all, I'd auditioned to play Cinderella. Only slightly horrifying that a colleague landed that role. But as I got into it, I had a blast. I threw myself into the character, relishing the chance to be over-the-top and ridiculous."

"Is that why you're so mean to Hayden? Because she got the role of Cinderella—the role you wanted?"

Paul lowered his head, unable to meet my eyes. "Ego is a powerful thing." He drew a breath. "But let's face it, I am the better actor. The role should have been mine."

I wasn't about to get into an argument about who was the better actor, so I asked the question we were all dying to know the answer to.

"Did you kill Joyce Harrison?"

Paul jerked, dropping the cotton pad he'd been using to wipe the thick makeup from his skin. "No. I did not kill Joyce. I would never harm any of my residents."

"But you agree she was blackmailing you?" Kade cut in.

Paul laughed, picked up a clean cotton pad, and resumed cleaning his face. "That? That wasn't real blackmail. Joyce thought she had a compromising photo of me. I let her run with the idea. It brought me in on their little operation, where I could keep a close eye on what they were up to."

"So, you knew about the buying and selling of drugs?"

"*No way!*" Paul looked aghast at Kade. "Seriously? They were peddling drugs? I thought we were dealing with books and candy and nail polish. That's why I let Joyce think she was blackmailing me, so I could monitor it and make sure they weren't getting into anything dangerous." He shook his head and ran a hand around the back of his neck. "Those crafty old women. I never suspected drugs at all. What are we talking? Cannabis? Cocaine?"

Dennis snorted and shot a look at his son. "Valium and Viagra, and small quantities at that."

"Okay. Right." Paul heaved a breath, blowing it out from between his over-painted fuchsia lips. "I'm going to have to report it. We can't have them trading in prescription medications. That's dangerous."

"Very," Kade grumbled, frowning at his dad.

"Where were you at the time of Joyce's death? And the moments leading up to it?" I pressed, unable to let go of the dawning realization that it was looking highly unlikely Paul killed her. I'd been so sure it was him.

"I was in a Zoom meeting with the board. Those meetings go for nearly two hours every month, and we were about an hour and a half in when we were interrupted with the news about Joyce."

"Was Hayden at the meeting too?"

"Yes. All our managers were." He looked shrewdly from Dennis to Kade to me. "But if you want to see that footage, you're going to need a warrant."

"You'll be hearing from the police," Dennis assured him.

Kade silently eyeballed the man for a solid minute before saying, "Thanks for your time. Congratulations on the play—may I suggest, to save yourself an ulcer, you simply tell the board? Why not comp them tickets? You may be surprised at their reaction."

Paul cleared his throat, looking sheepish. "Yeah, well, I'm probably going to have to since you lot can't be trusted to keep it to yourselves."

"I assure you, we have better things to do with our time than run back to Torres Place and gush to all and sundry about *your* acting career," Sylvia told him, eyes flashing. "You certainly have the hubris of an actor."

I couldn't contain a giggle, which I quickly hid behind my hand. "We should go," I said to Kade. "It's getting late." And we had a date with a dumpster.

I took a deep breath and steeled myself as we approached the grimy dumpster tucked away in an alcove at the end of the Torres Straight building. My heart was pounding in my chest as we prepared to sift through the garbage in search of the murder weapon. Eye drops. It was a risky move, probably fruitless, but some unseen force had been pushing me to find the eyedrops that had been used to kill Joyce, and I couldn't rest until I had. Was this a longshot? Absolutely.

"Ready?" Kade asked. We were dressed all in black, the flashlight apps on our phones the only light. It was dark at the end of the building. And just a tad spooky.

My earlier enthusiasm waned ever so slightly, but I nodded. "Let's do this."

The stench of rotting food and waste hit me as Kade lifted the lid, making me gag.

"Here, I'll give you a boost." Kade crouched down, interlocking his fingers together to create a foothold for me. Putting my foot in his hands, I pushed off, using his momentum to propel myself upward. I scrambled onto the top of the dumpster, my heart pounding from the exertion.

From my vantage point, I could see over the side and into the depths of the beast. The stench was overwhelming, and I could barely stomach it. But I forced myself to focus on the task at hand and dropped inside, beginning to search through the garbage while Kade vaulted over the side and joined me, our flashlights bouncing off the disgusting walls coated with goodness only knew what. Beneath my feet was squishy and moist, and I lamented the fact that I'd probably have to throw my sneakers away after this.

"Whatcha doing?" an inquisitive voice asked.

I screamed, tossing my phone into the air where it hit the side of the dumpster with a loud clang before falling amongst the bags of trash. It was a chain reaction. Joyce, who'd popped up next to me, had startled me so badly I'd screamed, which in turn startled Kade, who jolted forward and smacked his head against the side of the dumpster and was now cursing up a storm.

"Audrey," he whispered harshly. "What the hell?"

"Sorry, sorry." I waded to his side to check on his forehead, where he'd connected with the dumpster. "Joyce turned up. She startled me."

"Oh." He pressed his hand to his forehead, frowning when it came away with blood.

"Oh my God, you're bleeding!" I began searching for my phone so I could get a good look at his injury. An injury he'd sustained in a germ riddled dumpster. Visions of flesh-eating bacteria flashed through my mind, accelerating my heart rate and increasing my clumsiness. I flailed around, trying desperately to reach my phone, which kept sliding out of reach just when I thought I had it.

"Audrey!" Kade grabbed my arm and jerked me up. "Just stop. It's okay. I'm okay. It's just a graze. My tetanus is up to date. We'll clean it when we get back to Mom's." Then he leaned down and picked up my phone, handing it to me.

Taking it from him, I aimed it at his face, blinding him.

"Jeez, Audrey," he protested, screwing his eyes shut. "I told you, it's fine."

Joyce was peering at the wound with me. "He's right. It is just a graze. A good clean and a smear of antiseptic, and he'll be golden," she said.

"Hopefully not golden staph," I deadpanned. "This was a bad idea. What was I even thinking, expecting to find a bottle of eye drops in this? Eye drops we'd never be able to prove were the ones used to kill Joyce. We should go."

Kade stared at me. "You're giving up? Audrey Fitzgerald is giving up?"

"You're hurt!" I protested, pointing to his forehead, losing my balance at the sudden movement and almost falling over. Kade caught me, chuckling while he held my arm until I was steady on my feet once more.

"So are you, but that hasn't slowed you down any," he pointed out. "You know it's okay if we don't find out who killed Joyce. The police are investigating. They'll take care of it."

I deflated like a helium balloon with a slow leak. "I can't walk away and leave Joyce's spirit here. It doesn't feel right."

"Ahhh." Kade pulled me against his chest, wrapping his arms around me in a comforting hug. "You want to make sure she goes into the light?"

I nodded. It was what I did. Ghosts came to me after their untimely deaths, and I helped them cross over by solving their murders. To walk away with Joyce's murder unsolved felt... wrong. It felt like I was giving up, quitting, leaving her to fend for herself. And what if the police never found who did it? Joyce would be trapped here forever. No. That wasn't acceptable.

Pulling out of Kade's embrace, I resumed

searching. Joyce perched on top of the dumpster, chattering away about this and that. I'd long since tuned her out when I came across something interesting. "Look," I said to Kade, pointing to the bag I'd just torn open. Inside, sitting on top of the other rubbish, was a pair of blue nitrile gloves. The kind EMTs and first responders wear. They were crumpled, as if whoever had worn them had screwed them into a ball before tossing them in the trash.

Lifting the gloves out of the bag, I saw something wrapped inside, and I held my breath, looking at Kade. He aimed his flashlight at the gloves sitting in my palm and, with his free hand, slowly unfurled the fingers. There, nestled inside the glove, was a bottle of Visine.

"Oh my God," I whispered, not daring to believe we'd done it. We'd found the eye drops that had killed Joyce. I mean, they had to be... didn't they?

"Have you found something?" Joyce asked, then, before I could answer, "Oh, Tom wears gloves like those."

"Tom?"

"Yes, my son-in-law. Anne's husband. He's a paramedic."

And just like that, the cogs turned, and

everything fell into place. Shoving the gloves and eyedrops at Kade, I fumbled with my phone, bringing up the photo I'd snapped of the security footage from the café.

"Joyce." I gestured for her to come look. "Is this Tom?"

She nodded. "Oh, yes, that's him."

I turned the phone so Kade could see. "These two paramedics were in the café the morning Joyce died. Couldn't get a good shot of their faces, but Liam told me that this one"—I pointed to Tom— "bought a round of drinks for the ladies."

"That's right, he did." Joyce nodded. "Another orange juice for me. Pear juice for Sally cos she's a bit bound up at the moment and pear juice is good for getting the poop flowing. Oh, and Hazel had coffee."

"How did he know what you were drinking?" I asked.

"I always have orange juice at breakfast." Joyce shrugged. "Liam just repeated what we'd already ordered. But Tom didn't come over. He waved and sent us the drinks while they waited for their takeout order. I think they had another job to get to."

"I know how he did it," I whispered, eyes locked on Kade, the footage I'd watched flashing through my mind. "He ordered take out for himself and his colleague, then ordered a round of drinks for Joyce, Hazel, and Sally. Liam poured the orange juice and pear juice first, then made Hazel's coffee. While Tom was adding sugar or whatever to his own drink, he poured the eye drops into Joyce's orange juice, knowing that was what she drank for breakfast every morning. I remember seeing on the footage that he took a napkin and appeared to wipe down the counter. I think that was him screwing up the gloves and Visine bottle, and then he tossed them into the trash on their way out."

Kade carefully wrapped the Visine back in the gloves and shoved them in his pocket. "Was he wearing the gloves?"

I closed my mind, picturing the footage. "Yes, yes." I nodded. "He had them on when he came in, took them off at the counter."

"After he'd administered the eye drops," Kade said.

"Smart. Pretend like you'd forgotten to take them off, then remove them at the counter, use them to hide the Visine bottle, throw it all in the trash with no one the wiser."

"He knew the cameras were there."

I looked at Kade again. "Of course. He's smart."

Joyce, who'd been remarkably calm and quiet, spoke up. "Are you saying it was Tom who killed me? Tommy? My daughter's husband?"

"I think so, Joyce. I'm so sorry." How awful for her. The fact that Tom knew where the cameras were and had angled himself so they never got a clear shot of his face told me this wasn't some spur of the moment *let's kill my mother-in-law* type thing. He'd planned this. And as a paramedic, he'd have to know how toxic eye drops are when ingested.

"I was hoping it wasn't true," Joyce said, crestfallen.

"You knew it was Tom?" My voice shot up, echoing around us, bouncing off the walls of the dumpster.

"I kinda wondered," she admitted. "I didn't know for sure."

"Uh, maybe we could continue this conversation out of the dumpster?" Kade interrupted. "We found what we were looking for."

"Of course, absolutely." I tucked my phone into my pocket and let Kade boost me back out. Seconds later, he'd vaulted out and was dusting himself off by my side.

"How's the head?" I asked.

"Stings a bit, but it's fine." Taking a hold of my

hand, he led me away from the dumpster. "Let's go get cleaned up and work out a plan of action. Despite finding the gloves and eyedrops, we haven't proven that Tom killed Joyce."

"Joyce," I said to the sad ghost trailing along behind. "Why do you think Tom killed you? And why didn't you say anything before?"

"Because I didn't want to believe it," she cried. "I didn't want it to be him. But when you started asking questions, it got me thinking on not *who* would want me dead, but who would *benefit* from my death."

"Your daughter, for one," I pointed out.

"And her husband, by proxy," Joyce replied. "I left everything to Anne. And while I'm not a millionaire by any means, I have a nest egg tucked away that would certainly help them out. They're having money troubles, you see."

"Yeah, Anne told me you were helping them pay a few bills."

Joyce sighed. "She wouldn't tell me why money was so tight, just that it was, and she needed my help. And of course, I'm her mom. I'd do anything for my daughter."

"What's she saying?" Kade asked, ears pricked. "Was there money involved?"

"Joyce was helping her daughter out with a few

bills, giving her money every week, that type of thing. Anne and her husband were having financial troubles."

"Money is a great motivator," Kade half mumbled.

"Joyce." I swiveled to look at her over my shoulder. "Sally wasn't lying about the camera, was she? You really did ask her to keep it for safekeeping because you thought Tom was stealing from you?"

She nodded. "Sorry I lied," she whispered. "What happens now?"

"Now, Kade and I go get cleaned up because we stink of dumpster. In the morning, we'll talk to Tom."

CHAPTER NINETEEN

I was having the best dream. There were colorful clouds, all the colors of the rainbow, soft like candy floss scattered across the bluest sky I'd ever seen. And there was a wedding arch, strewn with wildflowers, and beneath the arch stood Kade, wearing a white suit. He turned, his face breaking into a wide smile. I stepped toward him. Only my feet wouldn't obey. Glancing down, I frowned. I was shackled to the ground, ugly metal bands around my ankles with rusty chains. I wasn't wearing the wedding gown I'd been in moments before. Now I was in denim shorts and a stained T-shirt.

Music began playing. My eyes widened in disbelief—it was Ben playing the harp. The wedding march, to be exact. Birds were chirping, then Bandit and Thor were trotting down an aisle of the softest, greenest grass dotted with yellow daisies. They reached Kade, who crouched to remove something from the cute little vests they wore. Light flashed against gold, and I squinted for a closer look. Was that a wedding band?

"Kade!" I called. "Wait!"

But he couldn't hear me. Seb appeared, wearing a hot pink suit, standing beneath the arch. Kade placed the rings on the open book Seb held, then turned back toward me. But he wasn't watching me. He wasn't seeing me. He was watching the bride, who walked so elegantly down the aisle. The bride with the pearls and the immaculate hair. She was like Snow White, with birds, butterflies, and small forest creatures dancing around her.

She stopped at the arch, and Kade reached out carefully, lovingly lifting the veil from her face. I was not the bride. It was not me standing beneath the arch, marrying Kade. It was Amanda.

I woke up screaming.

"Babe!" Kade shook me awake, and I lay there, dazed and horrified. I stared at him before slapping his face.

"Ouch." He reared back. "What was that for?"

"Marrying Amanda." Tossing back the covers, I threw myself out of bed and began pacing.

"I did not, nor would I ever, marry Amanda," Kade grumbled. "It was just a dream."

"Nightmare, more like," I huffed, rubbing my palms up and down my thighs. "Sorry for hitting you."

"Apology accepted." Kade flopped back against the pillows, and I walked around to his side of the bed, leaning over him to examine the graze.

"It doesn't look infected."

"Nor should it. I swear to God you scrubbed a good six layers of skin off in the shower last night. Not to mention the ultra-thick slathering of antiseptic. No germ would dare survive that."

"Oh good, you're awake." Joyce appeared, making me jump. Hand on my thundering heart, I spun to face her.

"Joyce! You can't just pop into our bedroom like that. What if we'd been naked?"

"But you're not." She pointed to my cotton shorts and faded tank that I'd slept in. "Anyway, that's not important right now. What is important is that Anne and Tom are at my apartment."

"They are?" I turned to Kade, explaining, "Joyce says Tom and Anne are at her apartment."

"They're going through my things. You need to stop him."

"Um, Joyce, they're going to have to pack up your apartment eventually."

"Yes, I know that. But I don't want him doing it. He'll hide away anything valuable and pawn it, I just know it. He's depriving my daughter of her inheritance."

"Come on," I said to Kade. "Joyce says they're packing up her stuff, and she's worried Tom is going to steal anything valuable."

Kade sat up, the covers falling to his waist, revealing his broad, chiseled, *naked* chest.

"Oh, my!" Joyce fanned her face.

"Relax, Joyce," I teased. "He has boxers on."

"What a shame," she muttered, eyeballing Kade with an appreciative gaze.

"Okay, enough perving," I said sternly. "Go back to your apartment and keep an eye on Tom. We'll be there shortly."

"Spoil sport." But she promptly disappeared.

"Dare I ask what that was about?" Kade drawled, stretching as he climbed out of bed.

"Just Joyce enjoying the view. She's gone now." Shimmying into a pair of jeans, I pulled a clean T-shirt over my head and headed for the door. "I'll put the coffee on." There's was no way I could face Joyce's daughter and son-in-law un-caffeinated.

"Be there in a few," Kade called after me.

I needn't have worried about putting the coffee on, for the enticing aroma of coffee beans led me straight to the kitchen, where Sylvia stood barefoot in jeans and a T-shirt not dissimilar to mine.

"Good morning," she greeted, not taking her gaze off the windows, half mesmerized by the view while she waited for her coffee. "Sleep well?"

"Yes, thanks. You?"

She blinked, shaking herself out of her daydream, and focused on me. "Did you and Kade go out again last night? After we got back from the theater?"

Darn. She'd heard us. I'd hoped we'd been quiet enough not to disturb them. "We did. Sorry if we woke you."

"I heard the shower."

"Ah. I had this theory, you see. I was convinced whoever poisoned Joyce did so at the café, only it had me baffled I couldn't find the empty bottle of eye drops."

"The guilty party could have taken them with them," Sylvia very rationally pointed out.

"Yes. I know. But anyway, through some inspired

flash of utter madness, I convinced Kade to go dumpster diving with me. To search for the eye drops."

Sylvia didn't bat an eye. The coffee machine beeped, and she removed her cup, standing aside to make room for me.

"And did you?" she asked. "Find the eye drops?"

"I believe we did."

Sylvia put her cup down with a thunk, the coffee coming precariously close to spilling. "You what?" she gasped. "Sorry, I don't think I'm fully awake. Did you say you found the eye drops that were used to kill Joyce?"

I nodded. "Uh-huh. They were wrapped up in a pair of gloves paramedics use."

"Morning, Mom." Kade gave his mom a hug. She returned the embrace, then leaned back, eyes zeroing in on the graze on his forehead.

"Care to explain?" she drawled. Now I knew where Kade got his drawl from—he sounded just like his mom.

"Banged my head in the dumpster last night." He shrugged off her concern. "It's fine. Audrey administered very thorough first aid."

Sylvia snorted out a laugh. "I just bet she did."

I blushed beet red, and they both laughed.

"Is Dad up?"

Sylvia shook her head. "Not yet. He takes a pretty heavy pain killer at night. Knocks him right out. Audrey tells me the pair of you found the eye drops?"

"Yeah, that's what I wanted to talk to Dad about. Can he contact his pals at the station and hand them in? They're in a Ziplock bag on my bedside table. Probably won't find any fingerprints, but you never know."

"Can't they lift prints from the inside of the gloves?" I asked, handing Kade my coffee and making another. "I thought that was something they could do these days."

"The problem is, the gloves could legit be Tom's, that he uses in his line of work. They don't prove anything one way or another. We need his prints on the actual bottle."

"He's too smart for that."

"Tom?" Sylvia piped up, eyes darting from me to Kade and back again.

"We think Tom Fraser killed Joyce," Kade explained. "Actually, we need to go. Tom and his wife are at Joyce's apartment now, packing it up, and we need to talk to him."

Sylvia reached for Kade's arm, stopping him

when he would have moved past her. "He's not dangerous, is he?"

"Relax, Mom, it's fine. Audrey and I are both trained professionals."

My chest puffed up like a bantam rooster. He'd called me a professional. I'd been called worse. "We've got this, Mrs. G," I said, hoping to hell that we did have it and Tom wasn't some sort of deranged psychopath, just your run-of-the-mill murderer. I bolted down my coffee, scalding my esophagus something fierce, but you know what they say. Hot coffee was better than no coffee.

At Joyce's apartment, a chill ran down my spine. The door stood open, boxes stacked in the hallway outside. Stepping over the threshold, I called, "Hello?" to announce our presence.

Anne and Tom were in the living room, packing up Joyce's belongings, carefully wrapping each item in newspaper and placing it in a box. My heart went out to Anne, who looked utterly devastated. Tom didn't look up, engrossed in packing the items.

"Oh." Anne frowned when she saw me, a flash of recognition pulling her brows low before her eyes moved to Kade standing behind me. "You're the lady from the garden. I'm sorry, I don't remember your name."

"I'm Audrey. And this is my fiancé, Kade."

"Detective Kade Galloway." Kade pulled out his wallet and flashed his badge. "Sorry to meet under these circumstances. I'm sorry for your loss."

Tom's head snapped up. "Detective? What are the police doing here?"

"I already told you," Anne whispered, voice heavy with grief. "The police called. Mom's death is being treated as suspicious."

"That's ridiculous." Tom resumed packing. "She was an old woman with a dodgy ticker."

My gut told me he was lying. There was something in the way he spoke, something in the way he avoided my gaze, that made me suspicious.

"Do we have to do this here?" Anne whispered, eyes glistening with unshed tears. "As soon as I stepped inside, I was greeted by the familiar scent of her cooking. Her favorite armchair sits empty, and her collection of bric-à-brac sits on her shelves. And yet the apartment feels colder, emptier, without her presence.

"Everywhere I look, I'm flooded with memories of her. I'm packing up her home, which in and of itself is an act of closure, but it also feels like I'm erasing a piece of her life. So, I repeat, do we have to do this here? Do we have to do this today, of all days?" A single tear overflowed and trickled down her cheek.

"Oh, sweetheart." Joyce tried to comfort her daughter, but of course she was incorporeal, her concern invisible.

"I know this is hard." I had to clear my throat to get past the lump. Or maybe it was the coffee burn. "But we really need to talk to your husband."

"To Tom? Why?" Anne's hand fluttered at her throat, while Tom straightened to his full height and glared at me. Kade rested a hand on my shoulder, and Tom's eyes tracked the movement, not missing a thing.

"About what? I hadn't seen Joyce since last week."

"That's not true," Anne softly corrected him. "You saw her at breakfast the day she died. You told me so. When they called and said she'd..." She choked off on a sob, cheeks now wet with tears. "When I called you and you said *what? But I only saw her this morning.*"

"Yeah, right, but that doesn't really count. I saw her from a distance. Gave her a wave. I didn't even talk to her—she was having breakfast with her friends. You should talk to those crazy old broads. I bet they're up to their eyeballs in this."

"Hazel and Sally?" Anne was horrified. "They're Mom's best friends! Of course they didn't have anything to do with her death. How can you say such a thing, Tom?"

"Uh, hello? Didn't they drag her corpse onto the golf course?"

"Tom!" Anne cried at the harshness of his words.

I admit, calling your mother-in-law a corpse in such an offhanded way was far from sympathetic.

"Sorry." He had the grace to look contrite. "I'm a paramedic. I see death all the time. I could have worded that better." He wrapped a comforting arm around his wife and hugged her. "Anyway, my point is, Hazel and Sally are the ones who saw her last. They had breakfast with her. It only makes sense .that it was one of them who slipped the Visine into her drink."

Kade and I exchanged a look while Anne pulled away from her husband. "How do you know that?" she whispered. "I never told you."

"Told me what?"

"That Joyce Harrison died from an overdose of tetrahydrozoline, aka eye drops," Kade said.

"That!" Anne pointed at Kade, her arm shaking. "That. What he said. That someone poisoned her with eye drops... I never told you that."

"Did you kill Joyce?" I blurted.

Tom looked at me, his expression a mixture of confusion and shock.

"What? No, of course not!" he exclaimed. Anne's eyes widened, and she took a step back.

"'Atta girl!" Joyce whooped, slapping me on the back, the icy shards of her touch temporarily freezing my lungs, so the breath I sucked in was raspy and loud, sending me into a coughing fit. I nudged Kade, silently telling him to take over while I tried to catch my breath.

"You were at the café that morning, correct?" Kade asked. "And did you, or did you not, send over a round of drinks to your mother-in-law and her friends?"

Tom cleared his throat. "Well, yeah. It was a friendly gesture. We didn't have time to stop and chat—and Lord knows Joyce loves nothing more than a good old chinwag—you know that's true, Anne." Anne nodded but didn't say anything and Tom continued. "Me and my partner stopped by to grab a takeout coffee, like I said, we didn't have time to stop and chat, so I asked the guy behind the counter to send them over a round of drinks— whatever they'd ordered for breakfast."

"Orange juice," Anne whispered. "Mom *always*

had orange juice for breakfast. Swore the vitamin C kept colds and flu at bay."

"It's true, it does. I hardly ever caught a cold," Joyce declared with a lot of head nodding and crossing her arms over her chest. "You should try it, Audrey. It'll keep you strong and healthy."

"Orange juice would effectively disguise the taste of tetrahydrozoline," Kade said. "A fact you would be very well aware of."

Tom looked wary, but he nodded. "Sure," he said, his voice guarded.

"Let's be real here. You had means, and you had opportunity." I'd gotten my breath back. "The only piece that's missing is motive. Care to share why you killed your mother-in-law?"

Tom looked at me, his eyes wide with shock. "What? I didn't kill Joyce! Why would you even think that?"

Anne half gasped, half screamed, making me jump.

"What? What is it?" I asked her, but she was staring at her husband as if she'd never seen him before.

"I can't believe it," she whispered. "Oh my God, I think I'm going to be sick."

"Anne?" She looked like she was going to pass

out. "Here, sit, sit." I cleared space for her on the sofa and pushed her down. "Shove your head between your knees."

"You kept asking me about Mom's will. What her assets were." Anne wasn't talking to me, she was talking to her husband, and that final piece fell into place. She'd told me in the garden how much they were struggling financially. And Joyce said she had a nice little nest egg that was Anne's inheritance.

"You killed her for the money," I said.

Tom's face went pale, and I could see the guilt written all over it.

"What I don't understand is why kill her? She was helping you out anyway, giving money to Anne every week to help with the bills. Unless..."

"Unless he needed a lump sum," Kade interjected. "You needed a substantial amount of money, and you needed it fast."

"Please tell me you didn't," Anne cried, face pale and wet with tears. "Tell me you didn't!"

Tom hesitated for a moment, and I could see the panic in his eyes. "I'm sorry!" He ran his hands through his hair and turned away, voice thick with anguish. "I'm sorry."

"Just tell us why," I said softly, needing to

understand what was so important that he had to kill his wife's mother.

"He's a gambler," Anne said, voice devoid of emotion, as if the life had been sucked out of her. "He promised he had it under control. That's why we were borrowing money from Mom."

I shared a look with Kade, who was already two steps ahead of me. "I'm guessing you were gambling away your paycheck every week, and then what? You borrowed money? Only you didn't win. You kept losing. And I'm guessing that debt came due, and you had no way of repaying it. Right?" Kade said.

"They were going to hurt me unless I paid up!" Tom cried. "Anne, I'm sorry. I'm so, so sorry. This is all my fault."

Anne burst into tears, long, loud sobs, her whole body heaving with the force of her anguish.

"Why didn't he just ask me for the money?" Joyce said, voice tinged with sadness. "I'd probably have given it to him. Maybe."

"Why didn't you ask Joyce for the money?" I dutifully asked, for Joyce had a point.

"Because of my stupid pride. And she would have lorded it over me every chance she got."

Joyce nodded. "Very true. I would have."

At least she was honest.

"So you figured the best course of action was to *murder* her? You realize the will has to go through probate, that you don't get your hands on the money immediately?" Kade pointed out.

"I was hoping it would be enough to hold them off before they broke my legs."

Kade snorted. "For a seemingly intelligent man, you're pretty stupid. How do you think loan sharks make a living? By charging exorbitant interest rates. The longer your loan is overdue, the more you owe. And for them to be threatening you with bodily harm, I'm guessing you are waaaaay overdue. Will your wife's inheritance even cover it?"

"Most of it."

From out of nowhere, Anne launched at him. One minute she was on the sofa, sobbing, the next she was screeching like a banshee and flying through the air, nails raking Tom's face while she kicked and punched at him.

"You selfish jerk!" she screamed, her voice so loud dogs three blocks away would have heard her. "I hate you! I hate you for taking her from me and then stealing what was mine. You are a piece of crap."

"Whoa!" I staggered back, taken off guard by her violent outburst. Not that I blamed her, not one bit.

"Go on girl, you get him," Joyce cheered her on. "Don't forget the knee to the gonads like I taught you!"

"Okay, okay, enough," Kade yelled, grabbing Anne around the waist and pulling her off her husband.

"What in tarnation is going on?" Hazel said from the doorway, Sally peering over her shoulder, eyes huge.

"Ladies, now isn't the best time." Kade grunted as Anne twisted and struggled against his hold.

"What are you doing to Anne?" Hazel charged forward, Sally hot on her heels. "Release her this instant!"

Hazel's concern must have penetrated Anne's rage filled outburst because she suddenly slumped in Kade's arms. He held her steady for a moment. "Okay?" he asked, peering into her face.

She nodded. "Sorry. I just... I just..."

"Saw red. I get it." Kade steered her toward me, where I seated her on the sofa again, this time keeping one hand on her shoulder in case she felt the urge to beat her husband to a pulp. Not that it wasn't justified, and not because I was concerned for Tom. More that I didn't want Anne accidentally hurting herself. It hurts when you punch someone —she could break a finger.

"I repeat," Hazel huffed. "What in tarnation is going on?"

"Tom killed Joyce," I said bluntly. "He needed the inheritance Anne would get to cover his gambling debts."

"But Paul Wilson killed her!" Sally blurted. "Didn't he?"

Kade and I shook our heads. "All Paul Wilson is guilty of is playing the part of an ugly sister in a play," Kade said. He looked at me. "You got this? I'm going to call it in."

"I've got it," I assured him, watching while Hazel and Sally got all up in Tom's business, demanding answers. Answers he spilled all too willingly. He was a broken man, collapsing into an armchair while the two women crowded in on him. I whipped out my phone and hit record, just in case he had a change of heart after he was arrested and recanted his confession.

"Well," Joyce said from beside me. "I guess that is that."

"Yeah," I sighed. "I'm sorry it turned out this way."

"I'm not. We got the truth. Anne finally got to see

the man her husband really is. A liar and a thief."

"And a murderer."

"And a murderer," she echoed. A flash of bright light filled the room, and Joyce gasped. "Is that for me?"

I nodded. "It's for you."

"Is it okay to go?" She took a step toward the light, then stopped and turned back, her eyes on her daughter, who was slumped on the sofa with her head in her hands. "I should stay with Anne."

"She'll be fine," I assured her. "Sad, but fine. Sally and Hazel will look out for her."

A big smile spread across her face as she looked at her two friends, currently berating Tom. "Yeah, they will. Say goodbye to them for me."

"I will."

With a final wave, Joyce stepped into the light. I returned the wave, letting my arm drop when I realized Anne was watching me.

"Was that Mom?" she whispered.

"Yeah," I whispered back. "She crossed over."

"I felt her go. Ever since she died, I kinda felt her around me, you know? But just now, there was this big rush of love, like she was holding me, and then..."

"She crossed. She's at peace."

CHAPTER TWENTY

"*Y*ou have *got* to be kidding me!"

"What's up?" Kade pulled the seatbelt low and tight across his hips.

"Dead Guy's here," I grumbled, snapping my seatbelt closed and glaring at the dead man in the seat next to me. "Are you following me?"

Dead Guy snorted. "Why would I follow you? You are the least interesting person I know."

"You don't know me," I grumbled.

"And I don't want to." He turned his head to look out the window, giving me an uninterrupted view of his horrific head injury.

Trying not to gag, I turned away. "Rude."

"Audrey? Babe?" Kade's hand on my thigh

reminded me we were not alone on the plane and I was doing it again. Talking to ghosts no one else could see.

"You know, despite everything, I had a good time in Chicago." I smiled. Meeting his parents had been a blast, and I genuinely liked them. Dennis had turned up with the local police to arrest Tom, and Sylvia had tagged along, eager to catch up with Hazel and Sally, who'd been more than willing to tell her everything that had transpired. Our last day in Chicago had brought with it gray skies and drizzling rain, so we'd spent the day playing board games and ordering takeout, and it had been perfect.

"Good. I'm glad." Kade leaned over and kissed me. "Just think, the next time we'll be on a plane, it'll be our honeymoon."

My heart skipped a beat. Our honeymoon. It was so surreal, I couldn't believe it was happening. I had a dress. We had a plan to deal with Amanda. My anxiety levels had decreased, and I was no longer stressing over the wedding. In fact, I was looking forward to it.

"I love you, future Mrs. Galloway," Kade whispered, resting his forehead against mine.

"Yeah, about that. How do you feel about being Mr. Fitzgerald?"

"I will be anything you want me to be." He didn't bat an eye, and I burst out laughing.

"No need. I'm more than happy being Mrs. Galloway." Entwining my fingers with his, I leaned back, paying scant attention to the stewardess conducting the safety demonstration in the aisle.

"You should pay attention to that," Dead Guy said. "Might come in handy one day."

"Why? Do you know something I don't?"

He hesitated. "Maybe." He disappeared before I could question him further, leaving me to spend the entire flight home gripping the armrests until my fingers ached. It wasn't until we were disembarking and I glimpsed him laughing his head off that I realized he'd played me.

"Ghosts can be such assholes," I whispered under my breath, following Kade to baggage claim.

"Tell me about it," a woman to my left said. I jerked around in surprise. There, standing next to me, was a bride. A bride with a big red stain on her pristine white gown and a gaping hole in her abdomen.

"Are you an... omen?" I'm not ashamed to admit I was horrified. Was she a sign that Kade and I shouldn't be getting married? For just when everything was falling into place and I was feeling good about things, she turned up.

"What on earth are you talking about?"

"You're wearing a wedding dress. You're clearly getting married. I'm about to get married..." I trailed off, leaving her to connect the dots.

To my surprise, she burst out laughing. "No, silly. I'm not a bride. I'm a model. And I was murdered."

"A model? Are you part of the bridal expo that's meant to be coming to Firefly Bay next week?"

"Oh, I see you've heard of me." She tossed her hair over her shoulder, preening.

"Erm, not you, personally."

"Oh." She waved a hand. "Well, anyway, that doesn't matter. Word on the street is that you're the ghost whisperer. I need you to find out who killed me."

"Word on the street? Like, do you guys have a ghostly bulletin board or something?"

"Or something. I woke up dead. I need you to find out why. Before another body drops."

"Before a—wait, what are you saying?"

"I'm saying I think I know who killed me, and they're going to kill again."

*Are you ready for book nine, **Life Ghost On***? *Order it here:* www.JaneHinchey.com/LifeGhostOn

Thank you for reading! If you enjoyed this book, I'd greatly appreciate your review.

You can find a complete list of my books, including series and reading order on my website at:

www.JaneHinchey.com

Join my newsletter here:

www.JaneHinchey.com/ghostly-newsflash

And finally, join my readers group on Facebook here:

www.JaneHinchey.com/LittleDevils

Thank you so much for taking a chance and reading my book . It's readers like you who make this journey worthwhile and fuel my passion for storytelling. Your support means the world to me, and I can't wait to share more exciting stories with you in the future.

xoxo
Jane

Are you a fan of the Ghost Detective mysteries? Sign up for my newsletter and receive two bonus Ghost Detective shorts!

www.janehinchey.com/ghostly-newsflash

READ MORE BY JANE

Find them all at www.JaneHinchey.com/books

The Ghost Detective Mysteries

#1 Ghost Mortem

#2 Give up the Ghost

#3 The Ghost is Clear

#4 A Ghost of a Chance

#5 Here Ghost Nothing

#6 Who Ghost There?

#7 Wild Ghost Chase

#8 Easy Come, Easy Ghost

#9 Life Ghost On

Witch Way Paranormal Cozy Mystery Series

#1 Witch Way to Magic & Mayhem

#2 Witch Way to Romance & Ruin

#3 Witch Way Down Under

#4 Witch Way to Beauty & the Beach

#5 Witch Way to Death & Destruction

#6 Witch Way to Secrets & Sorcery

The Gravestone Mysteries

#1 Fur the Hex of it

#2 Battle of the Hexes

#3 What the Hex

The Midnight Chronicles

#1 One Minute to Midnight

#2 Two Minutes Past Midnight

#3 Third Strike of Midnight

Clean Scene Inc.

#1 All in Vein

PARANORMAL ROMANCE/URBAN FANTASY

The Awakening Series

#1 First Blade

#2 First Witch

#3 First Blood

ABOUT JANE

Hi there! My name is Jane and I write urban fantasy romance and paranormal cozy mysteries, but let's be real, I'm just trying to figure out how to make my love for cats, coffee, and romance a career.

My hobbies include trying to outsmart my cats, getting lost in a good book, and pretending to be a plant lady (but really, I just have a lot of plastic plants).

In my free time, you can find me binge-watching true crime documentaries, planning my next vacation, and perfecting my "resting book face." I am also a big believer in the power of naps and have been known to take them at any given opportunity.

I also have a not-so-secret identity as an author of steamy and badass urban fantasy romance under the name Zahra Stone, so if you're looking for a little more danger and a lot more heat, check her out!

Find Zahra here: www.zahrastone.com

Find me (Jane) here: www.janehinchey.com

- facebook.com/janehincheyauthor
- instagram.com/janehincheyauthor
- amazon.com/Jane-Hinchey/e/B0193449MI
- bookbub.com/authors/jane-hinchey
- goodreads.com/jane_hinchey

Printed in the USA
CPSIA information can be obtained
at www.ICGtesting.com
LVHW051438121123
763715LV00040B/431